The Vocation of
BACHAN SINGH

To Brian & Jackie

from.

David

The Vocation of
BACHAN SINGH

by

David Money

Buckland Publications Ltd.
125 High Holborn, London WC1V 6QA

ISBN 0 7212 0901 7

Printed and bound in Great Britain by
Buckland Press Ltd., Dover, Kent.

CONTENTS

Foreword

Wartime anniversaries inevitably highlight momentous occasions stemming from decisions of politicians or generals, suggesting that active service involved incessant participation in dramatic events; whereas, for most of the time one's daily activities depended on changing relationships with a variety of unlikely characters, who shared transient anxieties, crises and occasional idiocies . . . trivia in relation to the broader issues.

This was certainly true of this gentle anticlimactic finale to the Second World War. It was downhill all the way, from a peak of high expectation to a doldrum of under-achievement, yet strangely rewarding. For in the twilight of that remarkable structure, the British Raj, this was the last opportunity to experience its unique ways of life, and to appreciate the mutual respect and affection between men from such different backgrounds.

Curiously, the figure about which it all seemed to hinge was no military genius, no Sahib, not even an NCO; but a humble, disadvantaged, yet generally cheerful character – Sapper Bachan Singh. In the end he, if no one else, was the achiever.

CHAPTER ONE

High Expectations

Often times one day is better than some times in a whole year
William Caxton: Tr. of *Reynard the Fox* (AD 1481)

So many of our days, no matter how rich in incident and momentary drama, merge into vaguely defined periods, defying all attempts to bring them clearly into focus. Yet here and there, for a particular reason, a single day can be conjured up in complete clarity. Half a century has passed, yet the last Tuesday of 1944 was such a watershed that the sequence of events in that prestigious corner of the Raj, the Poona District, comes back in precise detail, with all the flavours of life on the Indian Deccan.

Immediately behind were years of coping with the vicissitudes of jungle engineering. Ahead, in complete contrast, mercifully unrevealed, would evolve an increasingly unpredictable set of events, through which a small, cheerful, improbable "engineer" would wend his disruptive way . . . for *this* was the day that heralded the arrival of 40182 Sapper Bachan Singh.

Only the previous evening I'd returned to the familiar training area which had gradually extended over the parched countryside between three age-old villages. This dark bouldery plain with scattered acacias supported an ebb and flow of trainee Engineers sent from Headquarters, seven miles away, to be blended into active Companies. Here they were equipped; here their Officers Commanding competed and connived to obtain the most gifted craftsmen, the least suicidal drivers, and the pick of the equipment; and here their "Jungle Exercises Without Trees" severely tested our imagination!

I'd arrived with mixed feelings. At first dispirited at having to leave a companiable active unit; then intrigued by being told to form a Company with an unusual role; and strangely nostalgic about returning to the scene of those first encounters with the routines and traditions of the Indian Army. As the truck jolted its way along the familiar dusty, tree-lined road, remembered landmarks had rolled back the years. First impressions of India are unforgettable, especially for wartime officers making their semi-reluctant debut in the great sub-continent. As we'd bumped along this same rutted surface storms were building along the ragged crests of the distant Ghats, and a sudden downpour had released that pungent earthiness, unique to India in the rains.

Adapting to new ways of life had been strenuous, with deep concern at the speed and success of the Jap advances and the need to train so many so quickly – though countered by occasional nonsenses, for we'd arrived in time for the "*mendak gymkhanas*", those seasonal events triggered by the rains, when froggy communities occupying shallow ponds were at their most vociferous. As daylight faded, short peeps and intermittent honks gave way to a continuous deep rattle . . . matched by encouraging cries from the low bungalow Mess, as the field of carefully selected frogs was released at the centre of the chalked circle.

As we drove along, it all came back. I remembered the night Lidell-Smith was warned-off for shaking Heron-fodder the Fourth, his green-spotted competitor, in a glass of Nasik whisky, in the hopes of retrieving lost rupees in one super-amphibian leap; and, later, the demands for a dope-test as a squat brown entrant sat on his hand, throat nervously palpitating. It was all ridiculous . . . but therapeutic.

As the driver swung into the Mess compound I was surprised to see how little it had changed. There, across the lawn, was the long bungalow, the wide sweep of steps to the verandah, and the parched strip of garden with its few token marigolds and cannas. But, inevitably, nostalgia proved an unreliable guide to reality. This time there were no familiar faces. Khaki shirts and shorts had long given way to jungle-green battledress, and in the ante-room the chatter was all "shop". By the time I'd found temporary quarters any brief elation had completely vanished.

But Tuesday was another day . . . unexpectedly propitious, yet heralding that strange finale to it all, now forever associated with that singular character, Bachan Singh. It began with an atmospheric moment soon after dawn, the pipes and drums carrying sharply through the still crisp air, the mynah birds responding with their ill-coordinated chorus of hollow whistles. Suddenly I was glad to be back.

I remember threading through squads hurrying onto parade, NCOs shouting in time with the drum beats, and finding the relative peace of the new Company lines, a hundred yards or so from the river. Beyond, smoke was spiralling and drifting from a *langar* set among the neem trees, suggesting that at least there was someone to cook for.

So far only a handful of Sappers and a Havildar (Sergeant) had reported to Bhagwan Singh, the portly temporary clerk on loan from Depot, but an enquiring glance at the Register showed that, to a man, they were highly qualified craftsmen, a mixture of fitters, electricians, and bricklayers . . . an encouraging start. As yet there was little for them to do but tidy the lines; so, as Bhagwan Singh was anxious to collect the classified mail, I'd strolled down to the river to think things out.

The sun had been up about an hour and warm eddies rising through the heat haze brought a heavy smell of decay from reed-choked gullies in the bank of the sluggish river. In hindsight it's odd that the natural inhabitants of this unsavoury retreat would eventually deflect my intention to return Bachan Singh to the Depot as speedily as possible!

Meanwhile, there was a disquieting lack of information about this apparently unusual Company and what its exact role might be. When I'd arrived, Dawson, the G1, had seemed particularly evasive, even for him.

He'd simply said, 'We want you to form 725 Independent Field Company . . . No, I can't tell you why it's independent; the Commandant'll fill you in . . . By the way, you'll have to recruit high-Grade craftsmen, there'll be a lot of constructional work; probably with the help of the Naval chappies.'

Why "Naval"? . . . He'd ignored it.

Dawson was notoriously difficult to get on with. Impeccably starched, dark hair sleeked back, he oozed self-importance, but was so often evasive. All I'd managed to get out of him was that this would be an all-Sikh Company and, unusually, there'd be no British officers apart from myself and a 2 i/c. So who would that be? Dawson must have known, but he'd simply grabbed a sheaf of papers and walked through to the Clerks' office, mumbling over his shoulder, 'Bill what's-his-name; you came out with him I believe.'

It was still on my mind as I threaded through the clattering squads towards the Mess, and especially as I turned into the dining room and recognised the unmistakable booming voice of Bill Telford.

9

'Oh God! No! Not Telford! Anyone but Telford!'

He looked up from his plate and pushed back his unkempt tow-coloured hair. 'Martin!' he shouted. 'Great to see you! I hear you've got a new Company . . . Don't envy you. I've got 582, and it's bloody murder trying to get specialists. Decent Grades? I've been sent an absolute load of crap! Even the transport Havildar's called Ram Phutcar!' . . . A compulsive raconteur, given to addressing everyone in earshot, he would have been unbearable as a sole companion. Thank God he'd got a Company! The waves of alarm subsided; though, as it turned out, I needn't have worried.

Back in the lines there was a deceptive tranquillity. The Havildar had been improvising jobs for the arrivals, and several were white-washing the small brown stones demarcating the path to the Company Office, watched, impassively, by a stocky, grey-haired Mahratta herdsman, whose animals still grazed the Camp area. He stood motionless, holding a long *lathi* behind his shoulders in the crook of his elbows. Three bony buffaloes pulled at clumps of dry grass between the rocky outcrops. As one moved forward, raising insects from the dusty surface, a small white egret, perched on its back, planed down almost at the herdsman's feet. I wondered what he was thinking; for these mutually-dependent inhabitants of rural India and the three highly qualified technicians working lethargically at their menial task completely ignored one another.

As I turned up the white-fringed path, however, tranquillity became a thing of the past. Bhagwan Singh appeared in the doorway half-saluting, half-genuflecting in a manner appropriate for an HQ Clerk-on-loan, while behind, towering over him and trying to push forward, was a welcome sight indeed.

'Box! What are you doing here? I thought you were somewhere near Chittagong.'

'Good to see you, Martin! . . . I've only just arrived.'

This had already made my day. There was no-one I would rather have seen at that moment than Box. He'd been great to work with in the early days, but we'd almost lost touch. I'd no idea he'd come back . . . 'Thank heavens you've looked me up. How did you know I was out here?'

'I haven't looked you up, Martin, I've been posted to you. Got back to Poona late last night, and your clerk brought me out about half an hour ago . . . only found out this morning that you'd got 725: couldn't believe it!'

With his six-foot-six, or whatever it was, his long, lined face and thin-rimmed glasses, William Bosche, willowy to the point of being flexible, must have been a target for ribbing the day he'd joined up, straight from Cambridge. Apparently he'd become "Box" at OCTU, where the Drill NCOs, who had difficulties over names anyway, either thought it *was* "Box" or had regarded "Bosche" as subversive, and the name had stuck.

We'd come out together and shared an elderly *munshi*; though while I'd struggled with conversational Urdu, Box had almost effortlessly acquired a colloquial fluency. I'd worked with him long enough to know that with his quiet manner and almost acquiescent stoop went remarkable determination when dealing with things that mattered.

Meanwhile, in the shaded doorway the rotund obsequious figure of Bhagwan Singh was hopping about apologetically. 'Excuse me, your Honour, there is message. Commandant Sahib is wishing to see you at eleven o'clock. Group Headquarters is sending truck to Mess at 0950.'

'Right, Box, if that's the case, dump your kit, sort out a room, and do an about-turn. I'll take you with me.'

'Fine. I'd like to come. Unless there's anything I can do here.'

'Not really. We've only got a handful at the moment. We'll try and find *why* we're "independent", and see what HQ can do about transport.'

We arranged to share a bearer then hurried out, to find an 8-cwt truck from HQ parked outside the Mess, the Mahratta driver leaning against the tailboard. With a splaying of fingers and flexing of wrists, he was engaged in demonstrative conversation with the *mali*, who was slowly dripping water onto several wilted cannas under the verandah. The water trickled erratically from the nozzle, but sprayed fiercely from a leak further back, spattering the gardener as he bent forward, contributing an occasional, '*ji han*' or '*nahin, nahin*'.

Suddenly, aware of our approach, the driver, trim in shirt, shorts, and immaculate puttees, sprang to attention, saluted, adjusted his small neat *pagri* and, surprisingly, proclaimed in Urdu, 'It's not right for the mali to be asking me to mend his pipe. He is a lazy man and should seal it himself.' . . . A minute or so later, as the driver revved to overtake a small overcrowded bus stuttering along the road, Box said quietly, 'Of course you know he was really trying to sell the mali a roll of insulating tape.'

Still a good ear for the vernacular I thought, thankful that Box had arrived, and considering whether I ought to take him in with me. I wondered what the best approach to Dawson should be, and how much

I wondered what the best approach to Dawson should be, and how much we'd learn about what could be a very special mission.

The Headquarters administrative building was an impressive example of military architecture adapted to the heat. On either side of the central archway the high-ceilinged rooms were shaded by pillared arcades, above them a wide verandah running the length of the building. This rapid summons to HQ had strengthened the feeling that we'd been singled out for an unusual project.

'I won't come in,' said Box, 'but I'll see what I can do about getting transport.'

I turned in, out of the glare, towards the G1's office. Dawson was not at his desk, but behind, studying a huge wall chart of active units, was the tall figure of Honorary Lieutenant Mohammed Khan, the Subedar Major. He smiled and pointed his cane towards the connecting door. I was obviously expected.

'Come in!' To my relief it wasn't Dawson, in fact he wasn't there. The Commandant was bending over, sorting through a pile of buff-coloured files with one of his Q Staff.

Colonel Bentinck's approach was the exact opposite of Dawson's. His pale blue eyes never left you, but his habit of dipping his head and stroking his thinning hair made you feel that his suggestions were tentative, and that he'd rather hoped you'd go along with what he had in mind. In fact he knew precisely how you'd have to respond, but gave the impression that you'd done him a favour by agreeing with him.

'Ah, Shaw. You know Wilkinson. Do sit down. I'm sorry Bernard Dawson has a meeting, but I think I can give you the gist.' He dropped his chin onto his chest. 'As you probably know, I want you to take out a new unit . . . an Independent Field Company . . . to do some rather specialised work on HMS *Taltara*.'

'Aboard ship, sir?' This seemed a completely new venture.

'No, quite different. Taltara's a code name for one of the strategic atolls in the Indian Ocean. Overall it's under command of the Navy; but you'll be an Independent Company with admin through Ceylon Army Command . . . largely on your own, however . . . I gather oil-storage installation's going to be a priority.'

This certainly was not what I'd expected. The Colonel leaned forward and raised an eyebrow, 'Now, as I see it, and I'm sure you'll agree with me,' . . . as if I had a choice! . . . 'It's most important that we set you up with competent specialists who really know their job. All your fitters and welders, for instance, should be absolutely top-Grade. Dawson and Wilkinson here will see you get the people you want.'

It sounded better and better. But, stroking his hair, he leaned back. 'There's been just a slight kerfuffle, I'm afraid. We'd aimed to have you on the move early next month . . . When is it now, Wilkie? About a fortnight isn't it?'

'I'm not sure of the exact date, sir. Major Dawson's in touch with Movements.'

Assembling, training, and moving in a fortnight, with just Box and myself? I plunged in, 'Will we have help over the next week or so, apart from the HQ Clerks?'

'Ah,' said the Colonel, and paused, 'there are a few changes. For instance, you won't need many drivers and we're cutting back on HQ Platoon. It'll be a smaller Company than usual . . . that's right, isn't it Wilkie?'

'Yes, sir. I've amended most of the Indents.'

The Colonel paused again. He still hadn't answered my question; but looked up as if he'd just remembered what he was going to say.

'We're making it an all-Sikh Company and we've already earmarked some excellent VCOs . . . Viceroy's Commissioned Officers who've really proved their worth. You'll have Bulwant Singh as your Subedar. You'll find him great value. He's had lots of experience on the Frontier and I, personally, found him invaluable during the Eritrean campaign. Only two British officers I'm afraid, but the VCOs really are handpicked . . . What do you think about it Wilkie? Does that sound reasonable?'

It didn't; but then his "Wilkie" had turned the whole thing into a genial discussion, rather than an order to get on with it, and as soon as possible!

'Fine,' I said. There didn't seem to be any other reply.

'Taltara's hush hush, of course,' said the Colonel, getting up. 'The Movement Order will simply post you to Colombo; but we'll have more details before you go. There'll be a Company Inspection the day before you entrain. Dawson will help with the schedule. He won't let you down.'

Sobered by the last remark, but heartened by the prospect of a challenging job with an efficient Company, I walked into the midday glare in search of Box.

He was not in the main Mess, but in the billiards room with Tod

13

Davis, a regular BNCO, getting on a bit, but now commissioned. Long known as "Dai the Fix", he was a useful go-between if you wanted transport or whatever equipment he could persuade his wide range of acquaintances to part with.

'Back again, off again, I hear,' said Tod, patting the old Number One table. 'Been fixin' one of the legs. Got to get your priorities right! But not to worry, we'll start you off with a couple of 15-cwts, once you've sorted out your drivers.'

'Thanks, Tod,' I said, appreciating that Box had obviously made a rapid assessment of the most likely source of supply.

As we drove through the cantonment, with its regimented bungalows and leafy gardens, and threaded slowly through the rickety sprawl beyond, nothing appeared to have changed since we first came out. It seemed only yesterday we'd meandered over the potholed tarmac, past the small open-fronted shops, from which second-hand chairs and settees with split upholstery, harbouring heavens knows what, spilled out over the pavement. And there was the same small yard, packed with angular, dusty machinery; rusty lawnmowers leaning against the nearest pile of junk, their handles hung with tins of dried-up paint . . . exactly as we'd first seen them three years ago.

Its permanence was somehow comforting, like the erratic, jingling convoy of horse-drawn *tongas* the driver was reluctantly following. Jungle warfare was but a few weeks behind us, yet I think we both felt we were "back" . . . starting on something very different.

As we headed into the dessicated countryside I passed on as much as I knew, and speculated about our possible role on HMS *Taltara*.

'It has the makings!' said Box . . . What else could we have thought?

The dusty road was flanked by trees sheltering small family groups, squatting away from the road itself, waiting for the cool of the evening, their animals lying alongside or nosing along the storm-ditch. Over all was a sense of timelessness. I remember a feeling of quiet satisfaction . . . As it turned out, this unhurried ride was the ridge of the watershed. A few hours later 725 Company would be well and truly launched . . . the scene set for that unlikely engineer, Sapper Bachan Singh.

As soon as we arrived at the Training Batallion I walked to the Company lines to see if there were any messages. Outside the Office were three long, tidy rows of packs, watched over by a young Sikh NCO, who saluted rather uncertainly. From the barrack rooms beyond came a great deal of chattering. Nearly a hundred Sappers were being divided into platoons by two extremely smart VCOs standing by the door of the first hut, craning over a clip-board held by a Havildar, who turned out to be our senior Company Clerk, Prem Singh.

As I moved towards the Office path I realised that I'd overlooked the key figure. There on the verandah, quite still, in the proper stand-easy position, stood Company Subedar Bulwant Singh, where he could best supervise the move-in.

CHAPTER TWO

'His Name is Bachan Singh'

Experience with common sense
To mortals is a providence
Matthew Green: *The Spleen* (1737)

In 1916 seventeen-year-old Bulwant Singh had left his village in the Punjab to join the Army and serve, as his father had, in a branch of the Pioneers. On completing their service, his father and his uncle had been granted good fertile farmland, irrigated by Himalayan water drawn from the Chenab. Unlike most children in rural India, their boys had been weaned on tales of Service life and given a good basic education by ex-Service relatives. During the First World War, from their small village near Rampur, this military family had sent Bulwant Singh, two brothers and three cousins to serve their country.

After the War Bulwant Singh's military progress had been rapid. He'd been in sporadic skirmishes on the North-West Frontier, acquired an excellent command of English and, in 1934, had become a Viceroy's Commissioned Officer – a VCO.

As the Colonel had said, Bulwant Singh had been with him during the recent Eritrean campaign, and on his return as Commandant he'd brought him to the Depot to take up a senior training post. He could not have given us a more experienced Subedar, nor a more kindly one.

As I shook this avuncular figure by the hand, he seemed rather older than I'd expected . . . though to a twenty-five year-old any one of forty-six with a greying beard was getting on! But he was certainly impressive . . . *pagri* faultlessly wound, the level *pag* beneath, his beard neatly rolled and netted. The green battledress, bearing the ribbons of his

MBE, OBI, and campaign medals, had been well-tailored. I found myself pulling the peak of my cap straight!

After mutual salaams I led the way into the Office, but hardly recognised it. Clerk Bhagwan Singh had obviously been furnishing. The desk had acquired wire baskets crammed with papers and leaflets, with a small bowl of acacia thorns for use as pins. On the blotter was a neat pile of papers topped by a small sheet which said, 'For your honour's signature', a mode of address indicating Bhagwan Singh's clerical status, rather than any distinction of my own.

By the window a table-fan whirred briskly, cooling a bulbous earthenware water *chatti* and helping out the creaking punkah, turning erratically overhead. Dropping my clip-board onto the office safe, I filled a couple of glasses. Taking a tip from the Commandant, it seemed best to make our chat as informal as possible. Obviously I should let the Subedar know as much as I could about the move to Taltara and then, perhaps, encourage him to tell me what he knew about the Sikhs already posted to us.

He seated himself beside the desk, looking amiably expectant as I launched into an explanation of *why* we were forming this exceptional Company. Within ten minutes I realised he knew considerably more about the Company, its destination, and its likely role in the Indian Ocean, than I did. As he politely asked after his acquaintances in my Company in Assam and of those who'd served under Box, I began to appreciate that he knew a great deal about *us* as well . . . exactly where we'd been, how long we'd been there, and what we'd done . . . and probably how efficiently we'd done it! At no time did he refer to his own illustrious career, but began to tell me, as far as he considered he should, about the Sikhs, now noisily falling-in again outside the Office. I was already reaping the benefit of his years of military experience.

At this first meeting it was inconceivable that this exemplary figure could have an Achilles heel. Even if I'd already met the cause of this vulnerability, destined to induce so many headaches in the months ahead, I would have thought little of it at the time. Yet, unknown to me, this Tuesday had not only brought us an invaluable senior soldier, it had heralded the arrival of his nephew, Bachan Singh, anxious to uphold the traditions extolled by his relatives and, especially, to be a credit to his distinguished uncle.

Nepotism was part and parcel of life in rural Punjab, which supplied so many recruits. In the villages the old soldiers were apt to over-emphasise the attractions of Service life to the local youths and exaggerate the attributes of their young relatives to the Recruiting Officer. Nevertheless, successful recruiting depended heavily on the recommendations of these ex-Servicemen; and, as yet, I could only be grateful to a system which had provided the Corps, and now us in particular, with a remarkably gifted Subedar.

By the time we'd reviewed our likely procedure it was getting late. Crows were squawking in the trees behind the lines, where the newcomers were already gathering for an evening meal, and in the outer office the two clerks, apparently working cheerfully together, were hovering with our first Part II Orders. Obviously the Subedar already had the daily routine firmly under control.

Shortly after, Box arrived. He'd met Bulwant Singh leaving the Office and had also discovered that, while we were being sent to the atoll primarily to construct oil-storage tanks, we would also be enlarging causeways between the islands and maintaining the airfield and roads. It sounded great: constructional engineering again after years of improvisation. No wonder we'd need as many skilled craftsmen as possible. It wasn't a pipe dream. It was a really pleasing prospect after the uncertainties of jungle warfare and support engineering . . . On thinking back, we simply couldn't have believed otherwise!

Another crisp, invigorating dawn found us properly involved in the bustle and bull of morning parade. Yesterday's misgivings had been replaced by a touch of euphoria. The Commandant was obviously pulling strings to put a most proficient unit on the road, for already a sizeable intake was forming-up on the rough basalt surface which stood in for a parade ground.

The first thing was to get to know the VCOs – then together review the postings and concoct a timetable. Box was chatting freely with them, using Punjabi colloquialisms, but, with some justification, I suspected that the Subedar found my Urdu more laboured, for he addressed me in English so fluent that he could jest about Box and Pritap Singh, the tallest of the VCOs, being likely to "see eye-to-eye" as they worked together on the Q side.

The mid-morning meeting brought the first hint that we'd acquired an unlikely character. Box, the Subedar, Pritap Singh and the two Havildar Clerks were crammed into my small office, going through the latest postings and trying to see where we were short of skilled men. The

Subedar was in complete control. He seemed to know most of those on the list personally, and also what chance we had of getting those we wanted.

'There are only two Grade Two tinsmiths in the Depot. Binda Singh would be no use in a Field Company. We should ask for Hari Singh. We must also look more carefully for better fitters and welders. I will see my old friend Liaqat Ali in the Workshops' . . . and so on. He knew what he wanted, and everyone seemed to assume that he'd have no difficulties in arranging transfers . . . In view of the time factor this really was an encouraging start.

Feeling perhaps that someone else should contribute, Box said, somewhat facetiously, 'Make sure they've all passed their Swimming Test if we're going to join the Navy!' In fact there was something in this, for many of the Indian troops who'd gone to Eritrea in '41 had had no conception of an ocean. As they'd zigzagged their way across the Arabian Sea, the recently-trained MT Sappers had greeted the tactical tacking of their troopship with knowledgeable shouts of "learner driver!"

'They're all going to be experienced chaps,' I pointed out, 'and in any case they can't qualify for Proficiency Pay unless they've done a stretch in the river . . . But I know you're only joking, we're not taking raw recruits.'

'There is one, Sahib, who has only just completed his basic training and cannot yet swim,' said Bulwant Singh, quietly. 'His name is Bachan Singh.'

How the hell did he know that? I looked at the list again, wading through six Kartar Singhs and three Chanan Singhs; and there he was, half-way down – 40182 Bachan Singh. His Trade was shown as, "Carpenter, Grade III".

'Can't think why they've put him on the list, Subedar Sahib,' I said airily, with no idea of the tightrope I was on. 'As you pointed out, we can get all the Grade Two carpenters we want. He's only Grade Three. There's not much point taking a raw recruit. Surely it would be better if he stayed at the Depot and went into Workshops, and . . .', I added, 'learned to swim.'

The Subedar beamed back at me. 'He is from a good military family.'

His reply seemed rather inadequate and a little abrupt. However, there was no real reason for me to take it any further and there was a lot more to be done; so I left it. If we had to reject a carpenter to accommodate a good tinsmith, we had the obvious candidate.

CHAPTER THREE

A Hole in the Bank

Where he falls short 'tis nature's fault alone,
Where he succeeds the merit's all his own.
Chas. Churchill: *The Rosciad* (AD 1761)

Who can understand his errors?
Psalms XIX 12 (c. 350 BC)

It was obvious that a great effort was being made to set up an effective unit, for the quality of the intake was splendid. There was the intriguing prospect of work on an atoll. The push to remove the Japs from south-east Asia was gaining pace. What kind of work would we do? How technical would it be? We speculated at length. There was no way we could have predicted what would actually come about!

At times over the weekend the lines resembled a crowd scene from "Ben Hur", with borrowed handcarts raced along by pairs of Sappers, cheered on by labouring squads and shouted at by irate NCOs. 30-cwts discharged items technical and mundane alike – portable pumps, power-saws, bundles of clothing, and hockey sticks – checked in by the massive Pritap Singh and his Stores assistants.

Box was working flat out coping with directives from HQ, and querying Indents made out by Wilkinson long before we'd arrived. These seemed to show that the decision to send us to Taltara had been taken a considerable while ago . . . though the significance of this would only dawn on us when we reached the atoll. Meanwhile we had to get ready to move. We were far from complete and the time was short.

Clouds were building to the lee of the hills and it had become unseasonably sticky, especially in the Office, where the overhead punkah had packed up completely. I set about checking the few Company books already in use, helped by the invaluable Bhagwan Singh, overweight, slightly wheezing, but every inch an HQ Clerk. Regulations required us to keep about three dozen, but I was determined to prepare the minimum. It was not easy. Bhagwan Singh would come up with:

'Your honour has not yet a book for VD Register.'

'I don't think we'll need that for the moment, will we?'

'Who is to tell, your honour? Regulations . . .'

'All right, Bhagwan Singh, make out the headings. Is that all?'

'No, your honour, there is Register of Deserters Book . . . not yet on list.'

'No one's run away, surely?'

'Not all on posting have arrived, your honour.'

'Then they can't desert!'

'They are posted, and if not arriving, are deserting.'

'All right, Bhagwan Singh. That's about it.'

'No, your honour, we have not recorded list of books and documents being held in our possession.'

'All right, Bhagwan Singh, here's a blank book, write them in.'

'No, your honour, Documents Register is special book. I am bringing from HQ tomorrow.'

'Very good, Bhagwan Singh. I think that's it for the moment.'

It had become even closer. Debating "more air or more flies", I pushed at the window flap, admitting distant sounds of distress. I leaned out as far as I could . . . On the path to the river was a figure resembling the Hunchback of Notre Dame, doubled up and waving an arm about. A closer look revealed Bill Telford in a bush-jacket, struggling with a large piece of machinery. I ran, thankful to be outside . . . It proved to be an enormous pre-War accordion he'd found in a local bazaar.

'Martin, thank God! Help me with this strap, it's tightened across my back. Thought I'd take the old squeeze-box for a practice by the river, for tonight.' It was New Year's Eve.

That evening we visited the Platoons in turn, the celebrations a useful chance to get to know the Jemadars. Those variously talented engineers were so different in character; that lively optimist Bir Singh; earnest, dependable Mangal Singh, with full beard and ram-rod bearing; and the experienced, long-serving Arjan Singh, once an all-India hockey player. It was obvious they, too, were relishing the prospect of a mid-ocean venture.

At each *langar* we'd downed the usual tumbler of dark rum topped for supposed European preference with a finger of fizzy lemonade; and, though missing most of the Mess celebrations, saw in '45 in a contented haze . . . despite Bill Telford's raucous, even bawdier, Urdu version of the Ball of Kirriemuir, backed by his disintegrating squeeze-box.

With such an smooth, if hectic, start, there could well be time for a get-together exercise. Early next morning, on New Year's Day, Dawson rewrote *that* particular script. He and Wilkinson arrived unheralded, just as we were leaving the Mess.

'Ah, caught you!' he said, as though we were taking the day off. 'Thought I'd see how things are going. You'll be pleased to hear we've got your Movement Order – entraining at 1600 on the ninth, a week tomorrow. Bit of a rush, but can't be helped. Let me see . . .' He pulled a notebook from the top pocket of his immaculately starched bush-shirt and flicked through the pages. 'Due in Colombo on the thirteenth. You'll get details about embarkation when you arrive.'

'But that's only . . .'

He ignored it with a shrug. 'We've got no choice as far as the traffic people are concerned,' and then, blandly, 'There shouldn't be too many problems, but we thought we'd come and have a look-see.'

We walked briskly down to the lines, where Wilkie and Box took a more leisurely stroll to find Pritap Singh in the Stores. After a brief chat with the Subedar, Dawson stumped off to find where his driver had parked the staff car, taking me with him. Just before he left he loosed off two final salvoes.

'The Governor of Bombay's already back at Ganeshkind . . . the sticky spell's brought them up from the coast. Summer starts early at Government House! Sir John's coming in for Guest Night on Friday . . . three-line whip I'm afraid.'

God! That's the last thing we want, an official Dinner with all the paraphernalia of dressing-up and getting bearers organised . . . Bearers? Of course, we'd now have to find personal orderlies from within the Company.

He stopped as he was getting into the car and gripped my arm. 'By the way, to save time, we've arranged for a Company Parade and Inspection at 0800 on the day you leave. Should give you plenty of time to load up. Transport's already laid on. Details in a day or so.'

At the worst, I'd imagined the Commandant might opt for an informal visit the day before we left; at the best that any final Inspection would be called off, in view of the rush.

By Wednesday the skies had cleared. Aware that we were earmarked for something special, the VCOs stepped up the pace. Platoons switched duties in rotation, feverishly dealing with incoming materials, humping equipment and, with Inspection looming, fitting in Arms Drill.

The intake was nearly complete. Most were from active units, where Arms Drill was a very sporadic exercise, yet their performance on the irregular, drought-cracked surface was impressive. I'd just agreed with Mangal Singh that, being this good, they might as well get back to work, when Box appeared.

'It seems we've got a couple of problems,' he said. 'You remember the Subedar's non-swimming Bachan Singh, or whatever his name is? Well, he arrived last night with the batch that broke down near Yeraoda, and went on parade this morning with 1 Platoon. He's an extraordinary little chap, absolutely uncoordinated . . . looks like an overweight jockey . . . kept falling over himself.'

'It's difficult to march properly on this,' I pointed out charitably, kicking at the bouldery surface. 'It's remarkable how well they've been coping; in fact I think we can leave it at that . . . there's a hell of a lot to do apart from the Parade.'

'Exactly,' said Box. 'I thought 1 Platoon was coping well . . . which is why what's-his-name looked so bloody awful. Bir Singh was pretty patient with him, but afterwards suggested that the Subedar should think of transferring him to HQ Platoon and let him work in the Stores.'

'He'll still have to appear on parade, Box, whether he's in the Stores or not. Have you had a word with the Subedar?'

'The trouble is I can't find him. Apparently he's gone to collect a Religious Teacher, of all things! Prem Singh tells me we've got one on the strength. He's coming with us.'

'That's right . . . But about Bachan Singh. When the Subedar gets back I'll suggest posting him, if you like. He's a carpenter, isn't he? . . . Now what else is there?'

'Nothing much really. Just that someone's been nicking eggs. Pritap Singh's been keeping eggs for the VCOs in the ration store and they've been disappearing. Three went on Sunday night and another five last night, even though we've had a guard on the Store. They're extra to rations, so they're keeping them in the contractor's basket. Apparently there are now only fourteen instead of twenty-two.'

'We don't want a rumpus at this stage,' I said cautiously. 'Not while we're trying to get everyone together; not over a few eggs . . . though I suppose we don't want a villain about. Make sure the guard knows it's responsible for fourteen eggs as well as the King-Emperor's arms and ammunition! But don't let them make a thing of it.'

As it turned out, I was drawn into a lengthy interview with the Religious Teacher, Gurdev Singh, before I could tackle the Subedar about our non-swimming, non-marching Grade III carpenter.

Gurdev Singh's white beard was not netted, which made him look about twenty years older than Bulwant Singh. But a solemn bearing . . . No! Even the first glimpse surprised me – a bulky, white-clad figure half-sitting on Prem Singh's office chair, bent double and shaking with mirth. Opposite sat Bulwant Singh, equally amused. I gave them a moment before greeting the Subedar, who solemnly introduced us, and then explained that he'd had to negotiate Gurdev Singh's release . . . from what I was uncertain, though the ins-and-outs were explained in great detail with conspiratorial laughter, which seemed odd in a tough elderly Subedar and such a venerable sage. Apparently the Teacher would join us on the eve of departure, when he'd conduct a suitable ceremony before the farewell *tamasha* . . . which with Sikhs was likely to be a fairly bibulous feast! I jotted down the time, realising that the week ahead was rapidly filling up; then remembered the problem and drew the Subedar aside.

'Jemadar Bir Singh's not very happy with a new arrival, Bachan Singh, I'm afraid. He thinks he'll do better in HQ Platoon. Perhaps Pritap Singh could find room for him in the Stores? What do you think, Subedar Sahib?'

A moment ago Bulwant Singh had been laughing with his friend; but now, suddenly, he looked uneasy. This surprised me, for he had the reputation of being imperturbable, and this, after all, was a trivial matter. He thought for a while, almost looking through me. I could hear the lizards scuttering up the wall outside.

'It is best to do what the Jemadar Sahib recommends,' he said, deliberately. 'I will see that Bachan Singh is put in HQ Platoon.'

'Right!' I agreed cheerfully, wondering why he'd seemed so bothered.

The following morning I made a point of looking for Bachan Singh, and found him in the heavy equipment part of the Stores with two other

Sappers, removing grease from an earth auger which 3 Platoon wanted to use. I chatted to them all, trying not to single him out. Box was absolutely right. This stocky figure was decidedly bandy and had the slightly anxious look of a jockey at the weigh-in. He was obviously not very sure of himself and kept looking about, as if he'd lost something. He had very light eyes for a Sikh and his wispy hair was escaping from the sides of his pagri. Under the smudges of grease, he seemed a cheerful enough youth, but not exactly what we needed . . . Yet, oddly, something told me not to suggest returning him to the Depot.

Thursday saw us shuttling to and from HQ. There were the usual loose ends to tie up, and it was time to shed our shared civilian bearer and appoint personal orderlies. Box, on Prem Singh's advice, had already earmarked a large angular lad, Ajit Singh; which proved a wise choice, though he looked as awkward as Box himself. It dawned on me that it might be a good idea to train Bachan Singh. He might not be an imposing figure in the Mess, but once we were on the move he'd probably cope well enough.

In the afternoon, as an excuse for a break, I walked down to the riverside, where 3 Platoon was trying out the new portable pumps, raising water from an auger hole on the terrace, and rested gratefully on the rough-cut steps which served the ferry during the wet monsoon. On the far bank a small white shrine beneath its protective banyan was shimmering with reflections from rippling pools in the dried-out bed. Despite the grinding and squeaking behind, it was relaxing . . . Two minutes later Ajit Singh came lumbering up the path with a message from Box . . . 'Can you spare a minute to come to the Stores?'

Apparently Jemadar Pritap Singh was now very upset. No eggs had disappeared on Tuesday, but last night the thief had struck again. Four of the remaining five had gone . . . why not all five? It was very odd. Nothing else appeared to be missing.

'I'll have another word with the Subedar, Box. I won't get involved with Pritap Singh if he's in a state.'

'It's not so much the eggs,' said Box. 'He's up-in-arms about Bachan Singh. He gave him a short list of equipment to check, but apparently he can't add up. He's got the general idea, but it took him four goes to get the right answer. He really is bloody awful.'

'It sounds as though we ought to replace him.'

'I'm sure you're right. Yet, oddly enough, when I suggested getting rid of him, Pritap Singh was very cagey and said he didn't think we should. I can't think why. He felt we ought to find him another job. But what? What do you think, Martin? Surely it would be simpler to arrange an exchange? As far as carpenters go, it only needs a chitti.'

'All right, Box. I'll see what I can do.'

I took both problems again to the Subedar. His answers were surprisingly bland. In the case of the missing eggs this was to be expected. He, too, was anxious to play down a minor theft.

'The eggs are not important, Sahib. This is VCO's problem, but if I find who's stealing them, you shall know at once.'

Then I told him about Bachan Singh and said I got the impression that he was willing, but not really up to it. On this score I got absolutely nowhere. Again the Subedar seemed to give it a great deal of thought, but all he said was, 'You are quite right about Bachan Singh, Major Sahib. He *is* willing; he is very willing, and this is why Pritap Singh wishes to keep him.'

That was all. I could see that Bachan Singh was going to stay in the Stores, whether the Jemadar liked it or not! I felt I had to do something.

'Look, Subedar Sahib, wouldn't it be a good thing if I trained him to be an orderly . . . gradually, of course? He could still be a Stores Sapper, for once we're on the move his duties would be light as far as I'm concerned.' . . . Why was I doing this?

This time he surprised me with the warmth of his reception. He raised his hands and shook them gently. 'That is a fine suggestion, Major Sahib. It will be a great honour for him. I will arrange for him to learn all he can from the Mess bearers before we leave – he is very willing.'

As it happened the Mess Secretary was also concerned with bearers and orderlies. After Dinner he'd been briefing the civilian bearers who'd be at HQ tomorrow attending Guest Night. As we were leaving he called me over.

'I'd like some of the military orderlies to ferry dishes from the kitchen tomorrow night. Could you arrange for yours to help out? We'll lay on transport.'

'Only one,' I said hastily. 'We're sharing at the moment.' This was certainly neither the time nor place for Bachan Singh to start learning orderly duties!

After breakfast on Friday I was waiting for a truck to take me to Depot when Prem Singh appeared, out of breath, with a message from the

Subedar. We'd been through the day's activities together after first parade, but apparently the Subedar wanted to see me again before I left. Obviously something drastic had come up.

I found him standing outside the Office, looking pleased with himself, scuffing the dust with one foot like an excited schoolboy, surprisingly out of character.

'Pritap Singh knows who the thief is!' he exclaimed, indicating the massive Jemadar, who was standing by the path overshadowing Bachan Singh, hovering a pace or two behind him.

I wasn't sure that this *was* good news, or the right time for an exposure, but it had obviously cheered up the Jemadar, who saluted extravagantly and motioned forward Bachan Singh.

'It is Bachan Singh who has found him!' beamed the Subedar. 'As you so rightly said, Sahib, he has been very willing, and is a great help to Pritap Singh.'

Bachan Singh may have had little military training compared with the years spent on the land, he may not have been numerate, but the fields and canal banks about his village had given him a different kind of knowledge. The tiny feet which had scrabbled in the dust about the contractor's basket had left a pattern which Bachan Singh could recognise, as easily as the mongoose itself could recognise snake holes in a termite mound. He knew where to look as he followed the tracks from the corner of the Store across the edge of the parade ground and among the boulders. Once he'd appraised the general direction, he'd gone straight to the holes in the river bank and had found the broken shells by the bushy shrub where, a dozen yards or so from 3 Platoon's auger hole, the mongoose had his home and his family.

It was the Subedar's story and he made the most of it. Bachan Singh at first stood to attention, then relaxed, looking from one to the other as Bulwant Singh's English flowed over his head. Neither he nor Pritap Singh had contributed more than a head shake when, finally, the Subedar said to them, 'Sahib has much to do, but he is very pleased!'

I was, though I hadn't said so. I made amends with, '*Shabash*! Well done, Bachan Singh!'

The Subedar continued, 'This is a great day for Bachan Singh, for I have spoken with my friend Bapu More at HQ Mess and he is willing to train him as an orderly. Tonight he has his first duty. At the *Bara Khana* he is to help the other bearers and orderlies in the kitchen!'

Despite the rush, I departed to pass on the egg saga to Box before I left for the Depot. He'd been mildly sceptical about the idea of having Bachan Singh as an orderly and was unlikely to approve of his debut at HQ; but I also wanted to see if he'd take *arzi* parade in case I was held up. Friday was *arzi* day; the parade a commendable compulsory institution in the Indian Army, a sort of complaints session, during which any member of the unit could ask for an interview with the Officer Commanding and seek redress for any injustice suffered, or more usually imagined, by himself or his family. A clerk or VCO might translate or take notes if this were advisable, but need not be present.

On active service *arzi* parade, whenever feasible, was apt to become a weekly social hour, simply because this is what one did at that time. Many complaints harked back to life in a distant village and often involved quarrels between relatives. The reasonable ones were passed for investigation by the appropriate District Officer, hundreds, if not thousands of miles away.

On this Friday, with so many newcomers, there shouldn't have been many *arzis*, but Prem Singh had produced a long list. In view of other commitments, we decided to see only those prepared to put in a written summary, feeling that this might discourage the socialites and speed things up.

As it turned out I had no difficulty in getting back on time. Almost everyone had seemed unusually agreeable . . . partly, I suspected, because they wanted to relax before the Governor's Guest Night . . . and on my return there were only two *arzis* to follow up, both familiar scenarios. Prem Singh duly drafted notes to DOs in far parts of the Punjab, asking them to look into allegations that a village postman was demanding payment for delivery and, in the other case, that a tree had been illegally pruned by a neighbour.

This left more time than anticipated, though neither of us could raise much enthusiasm for a distant formal Dinner. Yet, as it turned out, the *Bara Khana* was a pleasant enough break . . . with only a hint of things to come!

Seated in the Main Mess, there was time to appreciate formalities lingering from the high days of the Raj. The long teak table, stretching the length of a cricket pitch from the centre of the High Table, displayed the regimental silver. Above it a heavy brocade swayed gently back and forth, rippling with energy imparted by a small punkah-wala, slowly moving his hand, or sometimes his foot, as he reclined in a cane-chair outside on the covered arcade; the transmission through ropes and pulleys as efficient as one might expect at an Engineer Depot.

High on the walls, between the tall windows, were brackets with wall lights, each bright area commanded by a single gekko, taking in moths and flies with a flick of the tongue. Sometimes one would make a short stabbing run; otherwise they remained motionless.

Apart from a few hunting trophies behind High Table, the plain walls, the proportion of the windows and the decoratively carved swing-doors screening the passage to the kitchen, gave the large high room a simple dignity.

Civilian bearers in regimental dress hovered behind the chairs, red sashes and belts with ornamental buckles over their customary white uniform. With each new course they moved to the swing-doors to receive dishes brought along the passage by the orderlies. To save some of the scuttling to and fro, a long hot-plate had been installed just inside the dining room, to the right of the doors. It was mostly used for occasional serve-yourself meals. We had one brief glimpse of Bachan Singh in the passage, looking reasonably well turned-out.

It was all highly efficient. I watched the Commandant incline his head towards Sir John, stroking his hair with that familiar gesture. He appeared absorbed in conversation, but at the appropriate moment the thumb and forefinger would flick at Bapu More, his personal bearer, for the next course.

All had gone without a hitch and a gentle buzz of conversation showed that the main course had been finished. A flick of the Commandant's fingers and off went the High Table bearers to collect the ice-cold mousse, always a popular sweet in these conditions. The senior bearer approached the swing-doors, through which a tray of sweets emerged held, perhaps inevitably, by Bachan Singh, who shuffled tentatively forward. At that moment Bapu More paused and turned away. He'd seen Colonel Findlay, at the end of High Table, put out a restraining hand. The Governor was leaning back to admire the Japanese sword which the Commandant would formally present to him after "The King-Emperor".

Bachan Singh hovered, undecided, looking left and right for a recipient . . . then, turning to his left, lowered the tray gently onto the hot-plate. Seeing his exit blocked, he stood in front of it, properly and confidently at ease . . . A moment later, Bapu More, looking in horror at the runny brown mixture, pushed Bachan Singh aside, seized a tray from the next in line, and in a dignified manner made his way to High Table.

As Bachan Singh, obviously perplexed by his rough treatment, made his way back along the passage, Box said, prophetically, 'He's certainly *willing* – but we could have problems!'

CHAPTER FOUR

An Intriguing Web

The last error shall be worse than the first
Matthew XXVII 64

On Monday morning, to my surprise, Jemadar Arjan Singh waylaid me after Parade and presented a sparsely-bearded, determined-looking young Sapper.

'Subedar Sahib suggests that I transfer Karam Singh to HQ Platoon. If you wish, he may act as your orderly.'

What had passed between the Subedar and Bapu More I never discovered; noting only that Bachan Singh remained in the Stores, with no further mention of his potential as an orderly, and that in his place I'd gained a most useful helper, with a mind of his own.

Despite the rush, amid the chaos of sorting, checking, and packing, we'd laid on "Training for Inspection", for though the intake was more highly qualified than we could ever have expected, most were from active service units. They'd learned the value of weapon training the hard way, yet could still find Inspection unnerving. All but the non-combatants, that is Teacher Gurdev Singh, the tailor, happily named Sewa Singh – and the three non-Sikh sweepers would be on Inspection Parade with full kit and weapons. The Commandant, known to require a uniformly good turn-out, was given to questioning the odd driver, storeman, or clerk on what he would do if he'd located a Jap sniper, or if a fellow Sikh went berserk and made off with the rum ration. So, over the weekend Sections had paraded in their best, brushed up their drill, rehearsed answers to likely questions, and got back into their denims as fast as they could . . . it was all go.

The following day, our last full day, the day of the Teacher's farewell blessing, Box confirmed the reason for the Subedar's particular delight at solving the great egg mystery. He was going over details of departure in the crate-ridden Office, trying to decide on the types and scales of rations for the journey. A hit-or-miss exercise, for though we'd thousands of miles to go no one seemed to know how long we'd be travelling, nor the precise route. As I peered over his shoulder, he pointed to a recent Army Memorandum:

'The rail ration is a monotonous diet, and will NOT be issued wherever arrangement to cook the basic rations can be made.'

It was true. The authorised rail ration issued loose was not very exciting – just the usual non-cooking substitutes.

'We'll be able to make local purchases, Box. The distance between cooking facilities won't be all that great,' I suggested optimistically. Though, as it turned out, we could have done with a Company Prophet rather than a Religious Teacher! . . . 'But how did the rehearsal go?'

'Not at all bad. The mock Inspection went well until one of them keeled over and several others began to sway in sympathy . . . it's all in the mind, of course.'

'No major problems then?' Feeling that at this stage something drastic was bound to turn up.

'No, not really. But I've discovered something we might have twigged between us.' He leaned back and shut the connecting door. 'I thought I'd concentrate on the usual disaster area, HQ Platoon. A reasonable turn-out; though their drill was pretty hopeless. "Port Arms" completely defeated Bachan Singh. One of the Naiks, Chand Singh, had a go at him, and in the end got him to stick out his rifle and pull back the bolt all in one go, then stand still.'

'He'll be all right on the day,' I said hopefully.

'I felt there wasn't much else we could do – apart from persuading him to report sick.'

'But what did you discover?'

'Well, afterwards I tried to joke about the "Port Arms" with Pritap Singh; as you know he's got a splendid sense of humour. But he took it seriously, and said he'd help Bachan Singh all he could, because the Subedar's family was very proud of him now he's on active-service. So I checked the Register. Our cheerful little storeman comes from Bulwant Singh's village. They're almost certainly related.'

No wonder the Subedar had been so edgy! He obviously hadn't mentioned a relationship in case things went wrong and I'd insisted on returning Bachan Singh to the Depot. I almost wished we hadn't found out; but reflected that once we were on the move he'd fade into the background. So ignore it, unless the Subedar brought it up; and keep our fingers crossed for the morrow. Box agreed.

During the early evening we joined the Subedar at the Gurdwara to hear Teacher Gurdev Singh deliver short readings from the Guru Grant Sahib, the Holy Book, moving his whisk back and forth across it as he spoke.

After the short address and the customary distribution of sweets we gave them time to prepare for the *tamasha*. The night was still and dark, and as we walked back spicy smells were already wafting from the Platoon *langars*, smoke drifting across the reception area, where pressure-lamps threw a bright white light over a detail busily arranging chairs for the VCOs and their guests from other units.

When we returned most were dressed informally in loose shirts and *chaplis*, some in games kit; though the Subedar, like ourselves, was in uniform. Garlanded with sweet-smelling frangipani blossoms, we formally accepted tumblers of rum, topped as ever with the finger of fizz. It seemed remarkable how these particular VCOs had established a well-knit community in so short a time, and how quickly we'd become familiar with their personalities. Perhaps there was something in forming so rapidly . . . allowing, in this case, for the Commandant's personal interest.

As the dishes circulated there was an easy formality between the Subedar and his guests and a mounting chatter among the groups of Sappers sitting, tucking-in under the neem trees. After a while the voices rose to a hubbub and nasal chanting began to drown the quavering sitar and intricate percussion coming from speakers in the adjacent lines. It seemed a good time to move on.

'Not a bad send-off,' said Box. 'I've got a feeling we're onto a good thing,' . . . blissfully unaware that, despite the invocations of Teacher Gurdev Singh, the passage to the atoll and our island sojourn would at times verge on the surreal; and that the least qualified of all would unfailingly emerge centre-stage.

The six-thirty parade was a brief one, accompanied by sunlit flights of pigeons which wheeled and settled, took off with a great rattle of wings, and settled again to wander about the lines, pecking at the remains of the farewell *tamasha*. The other ranks, looking commendably smart, were dismissed for a final polishing-up.

At 0755 a staff-car wound its dusty way from the Mess compound and delivered Colonel Bentinck, Major Dawson, a Captain Haynes, and the immaculate Subedar-Major, Honorary Lieutenant Mohammed Khan, resplendent in a pagri which raised his impressive figure to some seven feet. We walked across the basalt-black uneven surface to where 725 Company was drawn up under Box.

'I'm going to make it snappy', announced the Commandant. 'I'll first have a look at 1 Platoon and HQ Platoon, and then have a brief informal chat with the whole Company. Dawson and Haynes will go round 2 and 3 Platoons, and they'll be staying to help out a bit after breakfast.' He turned to his old VCO, Bulwant Singh. 'Come along with me, Subedar Sahib. I recognise a few familiar faces, but I shall need you to prompt me.'

The Commandant's Inspections were always thorough, and at Company level invariably jocular. His standard reprimand for a less-than-shiny rifle barrel was to tell the offender it was full of spiders or that he could plant millet in it, which usually went down well with men from a farming community . . . but he also made sure that the NCO knew about it, and for him it was a reprimand.

1 Platoon was faultless, so he spent a little while chatting with some of the NCOs who'd been in his old unit. I looked ahead at HQ Platoon. Even the Stores Sappers appeared well turned-out . . . smart, but petrified.

As we moved towards them, the Commandant closely followed by the Subedar Major, the order was given, 'For Inspection – Port Arms!' The Colonel tactfully ignored Bachan Singh's unorthodox manoeuvre, which at least finished in time with the others. But eventually, as he moved along the front rank, selecting and quizzing about one in six, he arrived at the kink in the line where Bachan Singh's posture tilted his squat frame backwards, as though he were trying to keep his rifle away from the Commandant's grasp.

With his attention drawn to it, there was no way the Commandant could have avoided taking the proffered barrel . . . he peered into it.

'Good grief!' he exclaimed. 'Look at this!'; and to Bachan Singh, who was watching him with bemused but interested anticipation, he barked

out, '*Dekko! Dekko! Tin, char makrian baithe hain! Makri ka sala hai.*
Have a look! You've got three or four spiders in the barrel! And a web!'

He turned to me with a twinkle. 'That's the last time I'll be facetious
on parade! Have a look!'

I squinted through the rifle, which he'd taken from Bachan Singh, and
sure enough several small creatures were slipping about inside the shiny
barrel, their long legs trying to get a purchase; a filmy web stopped them
from falling through the breach.

I looked at the Subedar. His face was a mask of despair. The
Commandant grinned at him, and Mohammed Khan grinned at him, and
I wondered whether they knew of the relationship . . . of course they did.

The Commandant's address was short and congratulatory. He drove
off in a sunny mood, obviously delighted that his well-known catch-
phrase had at last had some substance.

Jemadar Pritap Singh apologised repeatedly to Box about the rifle . . .
he'd personally checked it – he didn't say he'd actually cleaned it – but
during the break Bachan Singh had left it in a corner of the Store where
whole families of insects were looking for a billet.

Our final session with Dawson and the self-effacing Haynes, who was
new to the Staff, was a rewarding one. Dawson was at his efficient best;
checking the capacity of Wilkie's trucks and wagons at our disposal
against the personnel and equipment; getting Box to phone the railway
authorities to verify departure details; and finally, as always, firing the
last round:

'When you arrive at the station,' he said to me, with a wry smile, 'you
should go straight across and see the Movements Control Section. You'll
be O.C. Train.'

CHAPTER FIVE

'It is Problem of Delay'

Nothing happens, nobody comes, nobody goes, it's awful!
Samuel Becket: *Waiting for Godot* Act 2 (1955)

At least we hadn't to march to the station with bayonets fixed, wearing our sola topis, like the troops in the faded photos on the Mess walls. The move had gone without a hitch. Wilkie's fleet of trucks had collected the equipment and loading parties, and ferried the rest of the Company to the station yard. There was a cheerful atmosphere as they'd left the training area, with shouts of '*Sat Siri Akal*' exchanged with fellow Sikhs as the convoy threaded through the lines.

By mid-afternoon most of them were relaxing in the shade of an engine shed near the sidings, the wagons loaded, sealed and waiting to be picked up. Box was keeping calm control in the station yard, surrounded by a hoard of chattering children, fascinated by his height and his quiet acceptance of them. They kept a sharp eye on the railway police with their long *lathis*, and when they approached the small boys would scatter, dancing away, their shirts flapping outside their ragged trousers; though the tiny, solemn girls, with tinier babies on their hips, would continue to stand and watch every movement Box made. They ignored the squads of Sappers, who seemed as excited as if they were going on leave. Certainly everyone looked forward to shedding some of their responsibilities for a few days, or at least having to think only of eating, sleeping, and picking up a few luxuries on station platforms.

As the last of Wilkie's trucks drove off, I decided to check with the RTO about the duties of O.C. Train. In fact, I'd been O.C. Train before, and on that occasion, being blessed with well-organised detachments and independent officers with no problems, there'd been little to it.

As I made my way across the sidings, the train from Kalyan jolted slowly in alongside the main platform, creating the apparent anarchy which follows arrivals and departures at main-line stations. Vendors of tea and brightly-coloured drinks, shouting and gesticulating, jostled the vermilion-turbaned, red-shirted porters burdened with metal trunks, leather cases and canvas bed-rolls. Thirsty travellers struggled to join queues at the water-pumps, brushing past families squatting in groups, surrounded by cooking-pots, baskets, and bundles, and avoiding the old women sitting on coir mats, holding out thin arms and knotted hands. As always that priority for long-distance travellers, the provision of food and drink, varied with status: grey-coated restaurant staff bore stacks of pre-ordered containers to the first-class compartments, while in makeshift shelters at the end of the platform old men folded shell-lime and nuts into betel leaves for small boys to climb up and proffer the *pan* to clusters of white-clad figures on the roof of the end carriage.

It was a sudden transition from our cloistered community of fit and well-fed military to the reality of the struggles that went on about us. The anxiety on so many of these faces put our own concerns into perspective. The sweating porters, the fading garlands festooning cheerful and tearful leave-takers, the spicy dishes, the whole milling crowd, and the train itself blended to create the pungent flavour of India-on-the-move. Now we were part of it, anticipating the journey with a sense of freedom.

In the midst of it all I spotted a civilian railway official in a white sola topi laying down the law to two lost-looking Rajputs, and raised a hand to catch his attention. He thrust a paper at the larger soldier and pointed to the rear of the train. Then, steadying himself, he tunnelled into the crowd. The topi reappeared near enough for me to shout, 'Where's the RTO's Office?'

'I am showing!' he shouted and ducked into the mob again.

I eventually caught up with him and saw that he'd pushed open an opaque glass door and was addressing someone inside. He swivelled and dabbed a finger towards the sidings.

'RTO not here. He is seeing to Engineer Company, very urgent. Please be waiting.'

'I *am* the Engineer Company,' I replied. 'Thank you for your help,' and turned to plough my way back to Box, wondering if things would be as straightforward this time.

I needn't have worried. A portly RTO with a Brummie accent was running through a sheaf of instructions with Box. He greeted me with a brief summary: 'Through-run to Trichinopoly, then change to narrow gauge, and across the Strait from Dhanushkodi. We've listed all the ETDs and ETAs.' He glanced at his folder. 'You're due in Colombo on the thirteenth.'

'Saturday,' said Box.

'The train'll be in early by the way, which is why I came across. We'll hook this little lot onto the empty coaches reserved for the Company, they're already on the train.' He clipped his papers together and looked at his watch. 'If there's anything else I'll be in the Office. I'll get you to sign on the dotted line once you're entrained.'

'Seems straightforward enough,' I said. 'But there's one point. If it's as hot as this we'd like some ice. I know free issue doesn't start 'til April, but we could get some out of Company funds and perhaps top-up on the way.'

'I've seen to it,' said Box. 'The SMO can authorise free ice in the case of hardship.'

'Hardship?'

'Yes. I thought we'd already had our share of toil and sweat, so on Sunday I bearded the Batallion MO after a good lunch, hottest part of the day, and got him to phone the SMO's office for authorisation. It's already here – two maunds per eight men per day, and one for us.' . . . With Box and the Subedar, what could go wrong? . . . What indeed!

As predicted, the train came in early, flanked by two large engines, one hissing away at the front, the other, still detached, at the rear. An extra wagon with such immediate requirements as the unappetising rail rations, and those with technical equipment, previously sealed, were duly hooked up. Half an hour later the Company had settled in, the VCOs welcoming Box's ice, loaded into containers. Teacher Gurdev Singh, installed in one of the VCO's compartments, with the Guru Grant Sahib covered with an embroidered cloth, was obviously taking it all in his stride, for I could hear his deep voice and his shouts of laughter.

We walked along the train looking for our billet, followed by Karam Singh with my bedding-roll, and found a card with our names on the compartment door. Below them another had been pencilled in . . . 'Lt. G. S. Fouldes' . . . though there was no sign of a third occupant.

A contingent of Dogras, northern hill folk, who had obviously travelled a long way, occupied one of the coaches, the sepoys hanging out of the windows buying tea and fruit and shouting to others milling about on the platform. Two of them were precariously carrying a load of books and small bundles, which seemed to belong to a rather flustered officer in battledress and chaplis peering anxiously at the names on the carriage doors. As he caught sight of us, he hurried over.

'Am I in here? They took off the coaches for Bombay at Kalyan, so I've been in with the Jemadar . . . I'm Gilbert Fouldes. Do you mind if I dump these here, sir? I've got to collect my other things.' He relieved the Dogras of a number of canvas bags, a small tin box, a thin bedding-roll, and about a dozen thickish books, which he carefully placed on the long leather-covered seat beneath the window, then pottered off.

The compartment, with its dark wood panelling, retained something of its Edwardian splendour. Leather seats doubled as bunks, with a folding lattice frame to restrain the bedding, while padded leather-covered shelves hooked to the wall above the windows made it a comfortable four-berth sleeper. At one end a writing-table was folded against the wall, above it a chipped, spotted mirror, and below a stout wooden box, already filled with ice.

At the other end the heavy wooden door with brass handles and finger-plates led to the partly-tiled bathroom, which had suffered with time. The yellowing washbasin, as usual, had no plug, the mirror above mottled brown and almost opaque; but an interesting device occupied one corner. The downpipe which had once supplied a bath had been sealed off and a tap inserted four feet up. Beneath stood two kerosene tins, each with a perforated base and makeshift wire handle. We had a do-it-yourself shower! In fact, by wartime standards, there were all the mod cons and, surprisingly, all the lights worked.

Box was heaving his bedding-roll onto the near top berth when Gilbert Fouldes reappeared, carrying a map-case and another book bound in light vellum, with a tasselled bookmark dangling from it; but the RTO was trying to attract my attention, so I left them to sort out their possessions and establish territory.

As we walked the length of the platform the RTO went through the booking list. Besides the Sikhs and Dogras, there were groups of Indian NCOs going on various courses and a number of IORs changing, or rejoining units. There were also eight British PT sergeant-instructors, though they'd not yet put in an appearance.

We'd just turned back when there was a bang-banging of buffers between the carriages as the brake-van was shunted on behind our wagons, the second engine breathing heavily behind it. According to the list, a number of military and civilian railway staff would be travelling in the van. In fact a small group was already making its way back along the platform. I was about to go, when the RTO called one of them over . . . a slightly-built, bespectacled, earnest-looking Movements Control Havildar, curiously wearing a jaunty forage cap, a very loose bush-jacket and extremely baggy khaki trousers. He almost skipped across on his shiny black shoes and virtually skidded to attention.

'Major Shaw, this is Shankar Bhosle who's being transferred to Trichinopoly. He's been with us a year. If you have problems at any of the stations, I'm sure he'll be able to help you.'

'Thank you, Havildar,' I said. 'That's useful to know.'

He may have looked sloppy, but he clicked his black shoes, saluted smartly and about-turned as though on parade. As he tripped away down the platform, the RTO said, 'For Christ's sake, don't let him talk to you about rolling stock. He's a useful chap, but he thinks of nothing else. It's Trichy's turn to learn why Alastair MacIntosh increased cylinder capacity on the 0-6-0 that carried mica from the mines in Bihar!'

Finally, the PT sergeants arrived, nearly an hour late. As soon as the RTO let me know I walked along to see them. Within ten minutes of boarding five had set up a poker school and were already "seeing" one another on a tin box up-ended in the compartment. Next door three were stretched out, fast asleep. I didn't intrude.

It was nearly seven o'clock before the line of green flags started to wave. The two engines emitted a series of sharp staccato chuffs, and at last jerked us out of Poona. We swayed past the old cavalry lines, smoke drifting over the evening queue of carts at the paper mill, and began to leave behind the familiar outline of the surrounding hills.

As we chugged gently along Box helped Gilbert sort through his books, strapping most of them into the battered haversack from which they'd slipped, and stacking them on the spare upper berth. They were an interesting pair . . . Box tall, spectacles slipping, seemingly casual but utterly practical . . . Gilbert, almost as tall, but lean, with hollow cheeks, receding brown hair, and obviously highly strung.

I asked Gilbert about the Dogras. 'We're only a small detachment,' he said, almost apologetically, 'but I gather we'll be joining a similar one in

Ceylon. All I know is we're supporting some kind of construction project
. . . what, or where, I shan't find out until we get to Colombo.'

'Where've you actually come from?'

'We've travelled down from Jullundur. But we've been with a
Training Brigade in the foothills near Hardwar for the last month or so.
The whole idea, as far as I could see, was to endure as much organised
discomfort as possible.' He looked distressed at the very thought of it. 'I
went down with a tummy bug for much of the time. Simulated savagery
and squitters, what a combination! . . . It seems to have sapped me a bit
and three days travelling hasn't helped.'

The train continued clacketing gently along for an hour or so, then
slowed almost to walking pace as it ran into Dhond, crawling past the
small balconied houses, where tiny yellow oil-lamps and flickering fires
lit up the courtyards. The junction seemed even busier than Poona, the
dimly lit waiting-rooms packed. Box, wondering if there'd be time for
scrambled egg, attracted an official, but stumped by his repeated, *'Kya
dam hai?'* . . . 'What price?' had slipped him a few rupees and hoped
for the best. Gilbert said he'd already forced something down and
wasn't really feeling up to it, but had told his Jemadar to supplement the
men's tedious non-cooking rations. Pritap Singh, hopefully, was doing
the same.

We hurried back to see how the Subedar and the rest were coping,
picking our way between white-shrouded sleepers and family groups
squatting amid the red betel stains. A cloud of steam drifted along the
platform, as the now uncoupled rear engine made off backwards with
shrill hoots. I thought of continuing to the van to ask Shankar Bhosle
about it, just to get to know him, but caught sight of Gilbert leaning
down to take in trays from the station staff . . . curiously, it was curried
chicken and dal! Long before the short halt was up the trays were slipped
outside for collection.

Soon we were trundling eastward again, following the line of the
Bhima river, the lights of small stations flashing in as we continued to
rock slowly along, occasionally rumbling over gorges cut deep into the
Deccan plateau. But it was really too dark to see more than village lights
and the outline of the hills.

I flopped onto the lower bunk and followed the route on a
much-thumbed map of southern India, bought in a Poona bookshop.
Box, his knees drawn up, was reading on the shelf above, his height a
handicap when it came to bunks, though he had the enviable ability to

catnap anywhere at any time . . . out like a light, and back in circulation half-an-hour later.

I must have dozed off and Gilbert obviously followed suit, for his book fell from his hand, hit the floor with a thud and woke me up. I glanced at the title, "Essays of the English Association". Before we slept we'd established that we'd been near-neighbours at Oxford for more than a year . . . Odd that we should first meet travelling across the sub-continent in this small room, swaying with the gentle movement of the train.

Then suddenly it was light, and the small room was no longer moving. It seemed we'd only just stopped, the engine hissing loudly, threatening to get on the move again. I hauled myself up and peered at my wrist. Half-past five, we should be fairly close to Gulbarga and breakfast. I must have slept well, for I couldn't remember the clatter there must have been at Sholapur, which, even at our leisurely pace, was only three hours from Dhond.

Box, shifting about up top, leaned down to see out of the window. 'I think we're off again,' he said wearily. 'God, what a night!'

'What do you mean?'

'The stopping and starting.'

'What stopping and starting?'

'And all that clanking in between. We couldn't have been going more than ten miles an hour. Did you sleep through it as well? I know Gilbert did; I kept peering across at him.'

I twisted, pulled at the fly-screen-cum-shutter and leaned out of the window. The hissing had stopped and nothing seemed to be happening at all. After five minutes or so I slipped on a pair of chaplis, jumped down and walked back. It was a superb morning, with a yellowish light over the whole eastern sky. Stretching away to the south was a dun-coloured stony landscape with a village, perhaps a mile away, amid dark trees and a fan of brown fields. It was much like the Deccan scenery we'd left behind – but then we hadn't travelled all that far.

The group of railway employees milling about by the brake-van seemed to have been joined by a driver or stoker. I'd just identified Shankar Bhosle among the civilians when he shambled over and shook everyone with a thunderous salute.

'There has been trouble, Sahib. Dacoits have taken up track in several places. Train before us has been stopped and mail-van uncoupled. It is broken into and one guard is being injured. Oh goodness!' He seemed overcome with grief. 'This is at dusk last night and now unfortunate train is moved to siding. During night we cannot go through. More track may be gone . . . We are reaching this signal at slow pace, and now other trains are pressing from behind. We must wait for signal . . . It is a bad matter!' Anything disrupting the smooth running was obviously a personal misfortune, an affront to all involved with the railway. But he brightened up, 'I think we shall soon be moving.'

'Where are we, Havildar?'

'Is ten miles from Sholapur, Sahib. We are reaching Sholapur in half hour when starting.'

Which explained why I hadn't woken at Sholapur. Ah well! We could get breakfast when we arrived, and see how the delay had affected timings. It all depended when we'd be on the move again.

No one else on the train seemed concerned. Most of the Sikhs appeared to be sleeping, though a duty Lance-Naik and a Sapper with a pick-helve were standing by the wagons, a routine laid on by the ever-efficient Subedar, and Clerk Prem Singh was up, standing by the one open door. We greeted one another, but he didn't comment on the delay, so I hurried back to enlighten Box and Gilbert, if he were awake . . . Box was shaving, bending at right angles and squinting into the brown mirror. Gilbert had opened his shiny black box and was intent on powdering a leaf in a small porcelain mortar. The box proved to be made up of racks of tiny tubes slotted into an inner cover, which swung up to reveal a collection of minute jars and bottles in neat compartments. There were leaves in packets, seeds in tubes, powders in jars, and liquids of various colours, mostly greens and yellows, in the bottles.

'Homeopathy,' he explained, tapping the crushed leaves onto his palm, lapping them off with his tongue, and taking a swig from his water-bottle. 'Keeps you immensely fit and builds up resistance. You can treat such a variety of conditions. It's the natural way.' He took another swig from the water-bottle, then cleaned the mortar with a small brush. 'Father presented each of us with a kit when we left school . . . he practised it all his life.'

I thought of mentioning the tum trouble at Hardwar, but refrained. This was obviously something which meant a lot to him. However I pointed out that through the long history of the Raj the pukka Sahibs had generally gone in for brandy and port and a high Mess bill as insurance against Poona tum, Bangalore belly, or whatever.

Gilbert wasn't impressed. 'Long quaffing maketh a short life,' he quoted with assurance.

'But a convivial one,' said Box. 'They knew what did them good, even in Chaucer's time. "So was their jolly whistle wet y-wet" . . . wasn't that it?'

But Gilbert upstaged him by a good millennium with '"Give strong drink unto him that is ready to perish." . . . Proverbs Thirty-one.'

'Ambiguous,' replied Box. 'You could say . . .' But at that moment there was a high-pitched squeal from the engine. The party at the rear had boarded the van and a hand was waving something white from the window, so I looked up and down the train in case anyone had strayed, and was jolted backward as we pulled away amid plumes of acrid smoke . . . Soon the cotton mills at Sholapur were sliding by, and the town appeared ahead of us as we drew into the station.

The VCOs began laying-in fruit to supplement the biscuits and cheese of the non-cooking rations. I noticed Pritap Singh investigating smoke drifting from a lean-to down the line, and a minute or two later a familiar bandy-legged figure was cheerfully following the massive Jemadar along the platform, outstretched arms trying to keep a mass of mottled-looking chapattis in a sagging groundsheet.

The PT experts had yelled for the cha-wala as soon as the train had stopped and were beseiged by a crowd of vendors. I still hadn't made any contact with them, but there wasn't much need to, unless they had any queries or created any problems.

Another twenty minutes and we were off again, at a speed which would mean some two to three hours to Gulbarga . . . With the sun up the countryside had come alive. Men were toiling in tandem, swinging up skins full of water from the canals and turning them in sparkling gushes into the field channels. Bullock carts creaked their way along the village paths, and here and there a cloud of dust revealed a small, driven herd of goats. Above it all rose dark isolated hills, great bouldery mounds, quite unlike the flat-topped buttes further west. Some bore a small temple, others a low angular fort with crumbling ramparts.

Once the interest is held time passes quickly. I remained absorbed in the changing countryside, Gilbert was deep into a Tolkien article on Norse myths, while Box had found a metal bowl and was devising a way of filling it with ice and suspending it beneath the punkah, to obtain a cooling draught. He'd borrowed a cord from one of Gilbert's parcels and was busily making a sort of cat's cradle when we pulled into Gulbarga.

How long would we be here? I was beginning to feel we might not meet the Colombo deadline . . . and then? More immediately, I should make sure we could supplement rations at Raichur, a hundred miles or so to the south. I vaulted down; but stood on the platform, riveted by the sight of the great fortress rising beyond Gulbarga's domed mosques, kite hawks swooping over the dark, sinister mass which had long brooded over the struggles between Moslem and Hindu . . . At that moment Shankar Bhosle hurried by and thought we'd be leaving almost at once. As usual, he seemed well-informed, so I made signs to Box and the VCOs to get everyone on board.

Gilbert had managed to contact his Jemadar and seemed concerned about the Dogras. This was their fourth day since leaving Jullundur and he thought the sepoys were becoming apathetic. It didn't seem to fit in with what I'd seen of them on the platform at Poona, and the Jemadar seemed alert enough. Anyway, I was sure there'd be a decent break at Raichur, though perhaps I should have confirmed it, for once again we seemed to be rocking sedately along, occasionally slowing to a gentle clatter.

As the morning wore on the countryside became more dramatic, with deep *nalas* cutting across the landscape. Broken granite outcrops rose above the dry scrub, and there were stretches of desolate country with sandy-looking soils, in places white with salt.

Clusters of hamlets appeared where the land was more fertile, though even there men were standing on their wooden ploughs, shouting at the lean bullocks as they tried to break-up the crusted surface. This was their in-between season, heralding the renewal of the age-old cycle. Soon they would be celebrating Ugadi, the festival of the new year.

The sun was now high, the countryside shimmering with heat. A few field workers with large, loosely-wound head-cloths toiled on, though most were squatting in small groups under the solitary shade trees. Neat, upright women in purplish short-sleeved blouses and ankle-long skirts were making their way back to their village. Several turned to watch the train, but most took no notice. It was an irrelevance to lives governed by their immediate, familiar environment. That old dictum was unquestionably true . . . to understand India you should experience the patterns of village life . . . and I would have liked a more leisurely look at these closely cultivated valleys.

So perhaps it was Hanumantha, their propitious warrior god, who arranged it all. For suddenly the train slowed; then abruptly, carriages juddering, stopped once more, steaming away on top of a small embankment. As I leaned out of the window it began to pull away again, but then, with couples protesting, lurched to the left and ran slowly into a siding. Gilbert returned abruptly from the dragon-haunted world of Sigurd the Völsing and looked out, while Box followed me and dropped onto the side of the track.

About fifteen yards ahead an earth ramp led to a rough road, flanked by untidy piles of granite chippings. It looked as though the siding served a quarry. Just beyond the pot-holed road and a stretch of dry shrubs was a cluster of small stone houses with thatched roofs . . . a sizeable hamlet amid peepul trees and tamarinds, with limes and mangoes shading small vegetable plots. Beyond, the broad fertile valley narrowed between a wooded ridge and a steep granite bluff.

The railway employees were first out. Shankar Bhosle and one of the civilians went running off towards a low stone building which controlled the points to the siding and operated the signal, some fifty yards along the main line. One or two of the Sikhs were also climbing down, and we stopped to talk to the Subedar. Before I could reach the van, Shankar Bhosle was running back excitedly with the news.

'It is problem of delay,' he panted. 'We are being behind time and holding up most important freight train. It is ammunition train and must go through. Signalman says our train will go when freight is passing us, but cannot say "Go" until more instruction comes.' He brightened up again, 'There is also good news, Sahib. Freight train is pulled by new 2-8-0, only four months in India!'

'We'll just have to sit tight,' said Box. 'There's not a lot we can do. I'll ask the Subedar to spread the news along the train. I suppose we'll be even later into Raichur.'

Gilbert wandered up, wondering aloud if the heat were bringing on a migraine and, if so, what he ought to do about it. On hearing the prospect, he clasped the back of his neck with an agonised expression.

'Do you think we should get the men out of the carriages for a break?'

'It's up to you, Gilbert. I should give them the option, but I wouldn't let them wander down the bank.'

Meanwhile Box had told the Subedar about the delay and was pottering along the train by himself, chatting with the various occupants. Bulwant Singh seemed to have summed up the possibilities more quickly than Gilbert, or possibly Box made the suggestion, for a straggle of Sikhs, clutching shiny mess-tins, began making its way towards the engine. In fact the first arrivals were already sitting on their haunches, thrusting their tins under a steaming tap, held open by one of the stokers . . . it was tea-brewing time. The rest were being held back by Havildar Yeswant Singh to make way for two Sappers with an empty *ghi* tin, presumably for a mass brew-up. As the idea spread, the engine began to resemble a mobile canteen. Sparrows were winging their way from the trees and gardens and, accompanied by several cautious crows, were hopping hopefully about among the tea drinkers.

Several of the PT staff, sensibly wearing shorts with their red and blue singlets, began lighting-up, which meant tactfully reminding them of Sikh abhorrence of smoke and smoking. Fortunately neither Box nor I smoked, nor it seemed did Gilbert. As we stood chatting, Karam Singh made his way across with two mugs . . . soothing refreshment, for there was a growing concern that, with two connections to make, we were not going to reach Colombo by Saturday – and then what about embarkation?

We could only hope that the freight train would soon be through. It was the hottest part of the day, and in mid-valley dust-devils had begun to swirl across the dry shimmering fields, before losing themselves among the trees on the slopes beyond. Near the houses, sheep, goats, and bullocks were lying in shady thorn-fenced compounds, so that flies were a nuisance.

Box had asked Ajit Singh to find another mug for Gilbert; but by the time it arrived Gilbert had already procured a mess-tin of hot water from his orderly, and was adding Chinese Oolong herbs from a packet he'd produced from one of his haversacks. But his explanation of the beneficial effects on the circulation was interrupted by the welcome sound of an engine whistle in the distance. I looked down the track and saw that the signal had dropped. Back among the hills a plume of black smoke was billowing upward, suggesting that the train was not moving very fast . . . but of course it was a freight train and at least it had arrived, and there was the easily recognisable figure of Shankar Bhosle running gleefully from the signal box, trousers ballooning out.

'This is special train, Sahib!' He paused to catch his breath.

'Splendid!' said Box, downing the spare tea. 'We're on the move at last!'

'Please to be watching, Sahib!' . . . as if to an inattentive pupil; and turning to me, 'Only one engine of this type now working, and special carriages with all roofs flat-topped; built by Kitson, Bombay, like you have never seen, Sahib. Is coming from Wadi junction, from His

Excellency the Nizam's State Railway, only through-train from Hyderabad, very old service!' He almost danced with joy.

'This isn't the freight train?'

'No, Sahib, freight train held for track repairs. Telegraph is saying some delay.'

He dashed off, apparently to tell our crew of the approach of the venerable train, for the driver scrambled down. Like them, we stood and watched the ancient engine and the three box-like carriages, each crammed with forty or fifty passengers, go clattering by . . . but, unlike them, we didn't cheer or wave.

If the freight train were delayed, surely we could be extracted from the siding and moved to Raichur, where we could wait, if we had to, with more amenities for all? I set off after Shankar Bhosle.

'But, Sahib, there must be complete control for efficient overall railway system. Local train must run to time. Also Bombay-Madras mail is due. Ammunition train must also wait for this, then move safely with own priority. We are late, but must not interfere with proper service . . . we must all be patient, Sahib.'

Being marooned in this small siding was like being stuck between stations in the Underground – claustrophobic. Box suggested that we say nothing more to the troops for the time being, until we had more positive news of the freight train. I passed this on to the Subedar, aware that, anyway, he knew the situation as well as we did.

We also avoided telling Gilbert, though his migraine appeared not to have developed, for we found him stripped out on the lower bunk, reading and hooting with laughter, which seemed a strange reaction to dragon-slaying in the sombre northern forests; perhaps I'd glanced at the wrong bits.

Restless, we wandered back along the embankment. It was now past three. The men were returning to the fields. Slender girls were filling pots from a well in the shade of a banyan tree and carrying them back to the houses. A group of older women were scooping greenish-brown water from a shrunken pond, where a water-buffalo wallowed undisturbed, and were taking it to irrigate chillis and egg-plants in their family plots. Here we were, anxious to be on our way, tense with waiting, watching the unhurried activities of people responding to the seasons as they had over the centuries.

Just below us, two small girls were sitting in a bare sandy patch playing at pounding grain with stones, while another three or four-year-old swept the sand into piles. They chattered peaceably, watched by a tiny boy. After a while, he carefully eased two peanuts from the pocket of his torn shirt and gave them to the girls with the stones. He went leaping off, followed by the other girl, tearing at his shirt and screaming his name, 'Bhimsha! Bhimsha!' . . . When you're three and can't get a peanut, the feeling's much the same as being twenty-five and deprived of a train.

About four o'clock the Bombay-Madras mail swayed past. But there were still no encouraging signs. Our railway employees had gone down the embankment and were sitting under a tree. The driver was dozing by the track in the shade of the engine.

We rounded up the VCOs and decided that Pritap Singh should issue another non-cooked meal with its supplementary vitamin tablets and continue to brew in the ghi tins. There was still no sign of the freight train, so we walked along to check on the other occupants. The PT sergeants were slumped back, a few clutching soggy-looking cards, the others half-asleep. The only one taking a breather greeted Box with, 'This is a sod, sir,' but didn't seem particularly interested in the cause. The individual travellers appeared to have no major problems, apart from boredom.

Bulwant Singh rated this a minor hiccup relative to what most of us had experienced over the last few years, and of course he was right; but he wondered aloud, for the first time, how this might affect our movements by sea. We'd had no firm news about embarkation; though, again, there was nothing we could do about it.

About five-thirty there was sudden activity. The railway staff scrambled up the bank. Shankar Bhosle joined his friend in the signal box and the driver woke-up the stokers. Nothing happened for about twenty minutes, except that we appeared to be getting up steam. Then, unobtrusively, the freight train could be seen rounding the bend between the hills. As it slowly rumbled past, Shankar Bhosle ran the length of the siding to keep the locomotive in focus for as long as possible. The signal clanked up again . . . and that, for the time being, was that. We returned to the remains of the rations and the last of the tepid water from the Stores coach.

Large, foxy fruit bats, which had been hanging in clusters from the trees, were dropping off, opening out their huge wings and slowly flapping their way up-valley against a sky which had deepened from blood-red to purple. It was almost dark when we finally left the siding for Raichur.

The pi dogs began yapping and there was shouting from someone carrying a lantern; otherwise the villagers showed as little curiosity about our departure as they had about our arrival.

The train rocked slowly on to Raichur, stopping briefly just short of the station; but then, with the lumbering freight train no longer an obstacle, we picked up speed, passing over the long Tungabhadra bridge with a hollow roar. The pace increased and within an hour or so dull apprehension had given way to a surging sense of freedom.

It was a splendid starry night. Every so often a steely blue outline would catch our attention, and Adoni's ancient capital, high on its abrupt hills, unreal in the moonlight, excited Gilbert into gory details of Tipu Sultan's long seige . . . Some while later, as the train swayed its way southward, he added, still lost in the 18th century, 'Fourteen years after all that carnage the British got possession of it simply by a deal over the dinner table!'

It was the last I heard before we drew into Guntakal junction, stopping short once again to take on water. A general torpor had descended over the train's occupants. The Subedar posted sentries, otherwise no one stirred. We rumbled on through the warm night, with only one brief inexplicable stop at dawn, hissing steam in a strangely empty landscape, a pearly haze heralding a day of increasing heat and humidity.

At last we pulled into Arkonam, shed the individuals bound for Madras or Bangalore, and slightly augmented the rations. The PT group emerged en masse for the first time and managed to acquire four bottles of Bombay brandy to see them through the final long inland haul.

Before we left I encountered Shankar Bhosle again, and wondered what would happen at Trichinopoly now we were a day or so late. We'd made up a bit of time, but we were still anxious about the connections.

'Trichinopoly is Headquarters Movements Control for all south India, which is why I am to go there! All movement orders are coming from this Headquarters. No problem, Major Sahib. Orders will be given for quickly moving you to coast . . . to Dhanushkodi!'

It was good to hear such confidence, for Gilbert's translation of Trichinopoly . . . Tiruchchirappali . . . 'City of the Three-headed Demon' . . . had seemed somewhat off-putting.

By mid-afternoon we'd reached Erode junction, some eighty miles from Trichy, and the Subedar was wondering when next to issue rations. We should be in Trichinopoly long enough to arrange for a hot meal, for this was our main scheduled stop and Movements should have ensured a supply of solid fuel. It would, however, depend on the time now available, and this was absolutely unpredictable for we had to change onto the narrow-gauge line. Shankar Bhosle might well say, 'No problem!' . . . but we couldn't be sure.

In retrospect, the Trichinopoly experience appears a fitting prelude to our continuing descent from a plateau of high expectation to the reality of life in the doldrums . . . it was to be downhill to the Equator in every sense.

CHAPTER SIX

You Win Some, You Lose Some

Many false prophets shall arise and shall deceive many
Matthew XXIX 11

As the train reached its destination our small mobile community disintegrated. We'd hardly stopped before the PT sergeants, looking anything but athletic, made off into the City of the Three-Headed Demon in a haze of brandy fumes, and Gilbert, twitching with anxiety about time lost and a switch to the narrow-gauge, was trying to find the RTO. I was about to tap Shankar Bhosle's expertise for the last time when he appeared with a clone of the white-topied official I'd left in the office in Poona.

'This is Mr. P. K. Desai, Sahib. He is once with me in Poona. Station Master not here so, being Assistant, he is guiding you to RTO's Office. I tell him I am being of great service to you on journey.'

'Thank you, Havildar. You've certainly been interesting! Enjoy your new posting . . . Now, Mr. Desai, I expect you can show me where to go.'

'Of course, this is my job. First please be assembling on the narrow-gauge platform, at far end. We are shunting all sealed wagons onto the main line nearby. Then please to be supervising the unloading and loading. Dhanushkodi train is leaving in three hours.'

'What about my Dogra detachment?' asked Gilbert, anxiously.

'You are Dogras?' Looking at his list, tracing it down with a long, thin finger, 'You are Lieutenant Fouldes?'

Gilbert nodded. 'We're going to Colombo, and . . .'

'Then you will do same as Engineer Company . . . But no stores? Then please follow me to Dhanushkodi train.'

Gilbert again acquired temporary bearers from his Jemadar, and off they set like porters on safari, carrying his cases and boxes and books to where his detachment had assembled on the platform.

A moment or two later, Mr. Desai came hurrying back and with a twist of his wrist pointed out the RTO's Office. I left Box and the Subedar to see that the loose stores and rations were safely moved and walked across . . . hoping that once the wagons were shunted over we could break off for a hot meal.

It was a relief to hear the RTO confirm that transport had been set aside to move us to Dhanushkodi. The burly, gingery Duty Officer, Captain Pennington, had seen it all before. We were simply pieces being moved about the board, though apparently there could be problems with the crossing to Ceylon, for the ferry service still ran on a regular schedule. Our delayed arrival had stirred things up, and phone calls were going on between Pennington and HQ Movements, somewhere in Trichy itself.

Eventually he left a clerk to take messages and walked over to unseal the wagons, so that Box could get on with the unloading . . . On his return I listened, somewhat impatiently, to why he, Pennington, was turning down the chance of repatriation to stay on with the South Indian Railway. His fascination with the system seemed to rival that of Shankar Bhosle. Occasionally he broke off for staccato phone conversations which didn't appear to be getting us anywhere . . . It reached a point where I tactfully beat a retreat to see how things were going.

In fact they were going well. The unloading was almost completed and they were about to transfer equipment to the narrow-gauge wagons. At this rate we could soon fall-out, like the Dogras, who'd had relatively little equipment to deal with. I'd spotted Gilbert further down the platform, sitting on a crate, reading, quite undisturbed by a group of voluble Madrassis arguing fiercely and using battered black umbrellas to emphasise their points.

As I turned back towards the RTO's Office, Box came running over, pointing back to the sidings.

'Hold on a moment,' he said. 'There's a problem. We've brought four wagon-loads of equipment, but we're changing to narrow-gauge and we've only been given four wagons to load into. We're going to need at least one more. Desai says he can't help, he's only responsible for the station, and it's up to the RTO.'

'All right, come along, we'll ask him.'

Pennington was still on the phone to HQ and waved us to sit down.

'Good,' he was saying. 'Good . . . good . . . good . . . why shouldn't they? Soft-shoe shuffle in the sand . . . why not? Better than a holiday camp! Good!'

He put down the phone and looked at us in a self-satisfied way. We were obviously making the right moves on the board again.

'Have you on your way in a couple of hours. Everything OK so far? I'm afraid you'll have to bivouac on the beach when you arrive. Soft sand, warm sea . . . no problems.'

'There is a slight problem,' said Box. 'You've been asked to provide four wagons, but we shall need at least one more. They're smaller than the broad-gauge ones.'

'Of course they are . . . bloody hazard . . . happens all the time. You'd think they'd check on it, but they're always underestimating. All we get's a signal.'

Thank God we'd been more efficient in Assam! Surely someone should assess the capacities and make proper calculations . . . HQ Movements? The staff at the Depot? Pennington himself? Us?

'No problem. We've got eight narrow-gauge wagons on the rails. I'll make sure they're slotted in . . . two extra, you think? By the way, if your chaps want a meal-break now's the time. Take them over to the far end by the loco sheds, there are taps there for cooking and washing. I don't have to tell you to leave a guard on the equipment, and don't let anyone board the train before all the equipment's loaded.'

The only one to board the train so far had been Teacher Gurdev Singh, who'd managed to acquire several small steaming dishes, presumably from platform vendors. He'd been provided with a seat for the Guru Grant Sahib, away from the chain-smoking Madrassis wandering about the station . . . after all Trichy was noted for its tobacco and cigars, and had recently sent a selection to Churchill!

'You'll have to use your own cooking equipment,' said Pennington, 'and fuel.'

'We've no kerosene for the cookers,' I said. 'We'll need solid fuel.'

'Can't do, old boy. But a full firewood ration's laid on at Dhanushkodi. No problem.'

Problem indeed: there should have been firewood. Non-cooking again won't go down well, in any sense. Box passed the message, apologetically, to Pritap Singh and suggested funding supplementary purchases from whatever sources they could find. The VCOs had managed it, as we'd seen; but with so many it had to be non-cooking.

There seemed little else we could do. Feeling guilty, we rounded up Gilbert Fouldes and went in search of a meal. Pennington said he'd join us for a drink as soon as he could get away. As we passed through the fly-screen door, it seemed even more reprehensible to be tucking into chicken pulao while the rest of the Company was back on biscuits, cheese and tinned fish. Two long gins in a cool, commendably clean refreshment room, and a meal which left us replete, failed to clear the conscience.

After about half-an-hour, wondering where Pennington was, we decided to wander back; but at that moment the fly-screen door was flung open and banged shut again. Standing facing us was Mr. P. K. Desai. It seems trite to recall Jekyll and Hyde, but how else to describe the transformation that had produced Mr. P. K. Hyde-Desai? He'd been a quiet, solicitous, self-important but helpful Assistant Station Master. Now his nostrils flared and his white topi shook with his emotions. He stood stock still, glaring at me, and shouted: 'Your Sikhs! What *are* they doing? Whatever do they think they are doing? Who has given permission? I am taking this to high authority! No one is leaving the station 'til this matter is formally cleared up!'

Box pushed back his chair and stood up, looking down at him over the rim of his glasses. 'Tell us what has happened, Mr. Desai.'

'I *am* telling! The train will be held. No one is leaving station! Now *you* say to me why Sikhs are destroying the track . . . *why* they sabotage railway . . . *why* they are using axes. This most important junction. I am taking action!'

This had begun to sound serious. Leaving Gilbert to settle up, we manoeuvred Mr. P. K. Desai out of the restaurant and over the main platform. We followed him onto the line and across the track towards the marshalling yards, Mr. Desai straining ahead, trying to get us to accelerate. As far as we could gather from the streams of recrimination coming from under the topi, a militant band of Sikhs had been removing sleepers from the broad-gauge track and wantonly burning them. A station official had been sent to fetch Captain Pennington, but he'd not yet arrived.

The Subedar and Pritap Singh were there to meet us as we reached the sidings, and in the dusky distance by the loco sheds the whole Company seemed to be clustering around a fire, smoke rising and drifting towards us . . . my heart sank. Box began to stride towards the conflagration, picking his way over the sidings, closely followed by the small white-clad agitated figure of Mr. Desai.

'There seems to be some trouble, Subedar Sahib.'

'There has been a small mistake, but no one is to blame, though Naik Chand Singh was careless with instructions. Mr. Desai is very angry, for he is responsible to the Station Master. He wanted to address the whole Company, but I told him to talk first to me and then to report to you, Major Sahib, also to send for the RTO. I said I would investigate the complaint, but before he left he shouted at the cooking party and tried to put out the fire.'

'What have the Sappers actually done?'

By the time we reached the makeshift cooking-site and joined Box and the simmering Assistant Station Master the Subedar had put the whole thing in perspective.

Jemadar Pritap Singh had enthusiastically welcomed Pennington's permission to use Platoon cooking equipment . . . so if only he could find fuel! He'd told 1 Platoon to prepare to cook for the Company and HQ Platoon to scavenge for wood. The food itself was no problem – cooking *ghi* and a few sacks of *dal* and flour had already been unloaded and were under guard . . . so far, top marks for initiative.

Naik Chand Singh had seen a splintery old sleeper lying by the sidings way back, near the station. An old sleeper would burn quickly and fiercely! So off went HQ Stores Sappers for saws and a hand-axe.

'Cut it into thirty or forty small pieces!' he'd shouted after them as they faded into the dusk.

One could imagine the conversation between Bachan Singh and Joginder Singh on their way back with the saws.

'Which sleeper?' They looked around them.

'We must ask the Naik.' A hundred yards away, by the taps, the Naik was fixing the cooking-plates and sticking kindling under them.

'The Naik will not be pleased if we come back with no wood.'

'There is wood to spare on *this* sleeper.'

'Which sleeper?'

'All of them, they are sticking out beyond the rails'

'We could saw small pieces from this end. Look it's old and split.'

'You are right, Bachan Singh. You cut from that side.' . . . In no time they'd split it down into some twenty pieces.

'The Naik is saying "forty pieces".' . . . So off came the end of the next one.

Calling to the cooking party to come and help carry, they delivered their tarry wood to the grateful Chand Singh, and were sent off to return the saws.

Soon the two fires were burning fiercely, the metal plates getting hot, and squads forming up, chattering excitedly and anticipating a hot meal at last.

Meanwhile Mr. Desai, who knew nothing of Pennington's implied permission to use the site for cooking, spotted the fire and set off at the double. Aiming himself at the main party, he'd come across the shadowy figures of Bachan Singh and Joginder Singh collecting a few remaining faggots and the forgotten axe.

One look at the severed sleepers and the tell-tale axe was enough. He'd grasped Joginder Singh by the elbow, as though making a citizen's arrest, and yelled at Bachan Singh to bring the axe and follow him. Fortunately the first person they'd met was Bulwant Singh.

The Subedar completed his version of the assault on the South Indian Railway by the time we reached the fire, where the sight of blazing faggots had further inflamed Mr. Desai. He was once more threatening Box and the whole Company with detention until a formal inquiry could be carried out.

'Let's go and see exactly what the damage is,' I suggested.

Fortunately, at that moment Pennington arrived, having received a garbled version of events from Gilbert. His performance was admirable. Instead of firing questions, he at once gave Mr. Desai the impression he knew precisely what had happened.

'We shall have to look into this very carefully. I'm grateful to you, Mr. Desai, for acting so quickly. I agree with Major Shaw that we'd better examine the extent of the damage. I've got a torch.' It was now fairly dark, especially at the scene of the crisis. He directed the beam at my middle.

'If you'd come to the Office, Major, I'll help you prepare a statement. Would you ask your Subedar to carry on?' A crooked smile stood in for a wink. 'I'd just like a word with Captain Bosche, if I may. Then, perhaps, he'd stay with Mr. Desai until I've completed my inquiry.'

'Carry on, Subedar Sahib,' I said.

'Very good, Major Sahib. Carry on Chand Singh.'

Throughout the palaver, the duty cooks had quietly gone on preparing the *dal* and spices, stacking up the hot folded chapattis, and surreptitiously passing them to the squads sitting on the ground behind them.

57

Mr. Desai half turned, as though he might yet be able to stop the cooking, then smiled uncomfortably and took a step or two away from us.

Pennington walked Box away from Desai. 'He'll be all right. He talks absolute bollocks at times, but he'll calm down. While we're having a snifter in the office, take him back to the refreshment room and fill him up a bit . . . he's very partial to a drop of the old firewater! We'll join you in about half-an-hour.'

And so it was. The Company enjoyed the unexpected hot meal, though Nand Singh would get a rocket, and Bachan Singh and Joginder Singh would break even, with praise for their labour and initiative, and admonition for not making sure what their orders were.

Pennington and I had a whisky while he concocted a suitable face-saving, descriptive, non-condemnatory report for Mr. Desai. While in the refreshment room Box, Gilbert and Mr. P. K. Desai had enough juniper gin for the latter to recount at great length how such alertness was typical of the work he'd done over the years, which had at last earned him promotion to Acting-Assistant Station Master.

When the train left the quiet platform, just before midnight, ginger Pennington was standing by the Parcels Office, looking as if he'd seen it all before. Mr. P. K. Desai was unsteadily waving a green lamp and happily blowing his whistle with the rest of them.

As we pulled away from the junction Gilbert and his parcels and books were again sharing a compartment with his Jemadar, while Box and I stretched out on the torn leather seats of the non-sleeper. Whether I was supposed to be O.C. Train again I never discovered. This time, as we jogged our way towards the coast, its only passengers were 725 Company and the Dogra detachment.

I woke at Madurai and saw that the whole character of the landscape had changed as we'd moved eastward. There were palms among the padi fields and about the villages. Among the dark-tiled houses were temples with pyramid-shaped *gopurams*, too shadowy in the moonlight to pick out the details of their intricate carvings. The air was humid again and slowly moving masses of bright, moonlit cumulus cast grey shadows across the fields. The coconut palms gave a softer look to the countryside. Seen from the railway, it was peacefully beautiful, and gave me the feeling that we were now back on course.

It was barely light when we reached the coast and crawled slowly along the viaduct to Rameswaram island. The train dawdled through a dry landscape of thornbush and umbrella trees, for this long finger pointing towards Ceylon catches little of the monsoon rain, and storm waters sink into its pervious rocks. Through the fringe of palms the sea glittered with an early morning sheen.

We'd left on Wednesday and it was now Saturday; but at last we were leaving India, about to break new ground, impatient to reach the atoll and work together on whatever we'd been specially formed to do.

This time everything fell into place. At Dhanushkodi the heat and humidity were tempered by a strong breeze. The equipment was carefully unloaded and stacked ready for trans-shipment, and there was no need to hurry. Morning on the beach, and indeed the sea itself, were new experiences for many of them. This time Pritap Singh drew fuel with the rations, and soon the queues in the cooking area under the palms brought to mind ginger Pennington's "holiday camp".

By three in the afternoon we'd boarded and the ferry was nosing its way through the shallow blue-green waters, moving steadily towards Talaimannar, in the lee of the seven islands of Adam's Bridge, with Gurdev Singh and the Holy Book settled in the prow, where fumes from the funnel and smoke from the other Indian troops would not defile it.

As the coastline receded Gilbert Fouldes reappeared, swinging along the deck, seemingly in good spirits. He confided that he'd taken a small dose of arsenic after his morning constitutional, explaining that this not only toned him up but helped keep his hair in good condition. Once again I hadn't the heart to comment on his receding hairline or the incipient patch at the back.

Two hours later we'd docked at Talaimannar. With troops and equipment smoothly disembarked, and Colombo just a few hours to the south, we were almost a step from the atoll. We'd authority to start loading as soon as the train arrived. Then time for a meal before leaving, close on midnight. I checked the route. After crossing the long Mannar island, we'd run inland and swing southwards, skirting the highlands, avoiding coastal flats and creeks . . . Only there *was* no train.

Once again there was nothing we could do about it. Due in from Trincomalee five hours ago, it had been derailed at Gal Oya junction in mid-island, the engine in much the same position as the Reclining Buddha of Gal Vahera, a few miles away. It would need a mobile crane to upright it, and some of the derailed carriages were blocking the track.

There now seemed little hope of leaving until another train arrived from Colombo late on Sunday. The RTO, as matter-of-fact as Pennington, thought we might be away on Monday morning, or maybe not.

We passed the late evening on the shore, looking back across the Strait . . . After the luxury of hot meals, it was back to non-cooking rations, opening tins . . . and a night on the beach.

The sky was milky, with long streamers of high cloud radiating from somewhere to the south. The spicy breeze had given way to a stronger, gustier wind. We passed word around that it would be foolish to sit or bivouac directly beneath the swaying clusters of green coconuts, coupled with a warning of the effects of sand on small arms. As it began to get dark, rain appeared to be falling from high sheets of cloud, though only a few drops spattered onto the sand. It was almost as though the weather was orchestrating our misfortunes . . . from the sunny optimism of Dhanushkodi to the threatening gloom of Talaimannar. As a precaution, the Subedar sent a party to unpack and issue monsoon-capes . . . It was a rough bivouac.

Sunday, the day after we were due in Colombo, came and went. It was still threatening rain and very sticky. Frustrated, we spent some time swimming, to cool off. Once more we were in limbo, and once again it was depressing to be stuck in a wasteland with nothing to do; though word was we'd be leaving early Monday morning. Gilbert, on the other hand, seemed to enjoy the delay. As he gazed across the Strait, he professed to be overcome by a sense of place and history.

'I have a vivid picture,' he said, 'of Mahendra crossing this same stretch two thousand years ago, carrying in his mind the Buddhist canonical books, which he was to pass on by word of mouth.'

Box said he had a vivid picture of missing transport to the atoll . . . though we still didn't know when we were due to embark.

On Monday morning, with orders to entrain at 0900 hours, the Subedar had laid on an early parade. Just after six, refreshed by an early swim, we walked onto the rough sandy clearing standing-in for a parade ground. Bulwant Singh, as immaculate as ever, drew the Company up for Reports.

'One Platoon present and correct, Sahib!'
'Two Platoon present and correct, Sahib!'
'Three Platoon present and correct, Sahib!'
'HQ Platoon . . . one bayonet missing, Sahib!'

Before the Subedar walked over to Pritap Singh, I could have bet whose it was, and could only feel sorry for him when he formally reported, 'One bayonet has been lost by Bachan Singh. We know where he lost it. I will send a search party. Permission to dismiss, Sahib?'

The sand was silvery and soft and deep. It was also much trodden. Bachan Singh had used his bayonet to open fruit tins and had forgotten to replace it. We never found it, but wrote up "informal" Court of Inquiry proceedings, just in case!

* * *

In February 1978 our train from Colombo pulled into Talaimannar. Outside the station a slim Tamil girl offered us coconuts – splitting them with an old Army bayonet. But then the coconuts we'd bought on the road to Galle the week before had been opened with the help of an old Army bayonet . . . It would have been too much of a coincidence.

* * *

We left an hour late, puffing and chugging-along under a leaden sky across a dreary waste, the dry baobab country about Mannar. By the time we'd passed through Maho, somewhere near halfway, rain was lashing the carriages and blotting out the wooded hillsides.

By late afternoon we reached Colombo, the city steaming in the aftermath of the storms. Even standing, watching the equipment being transferred to the trucks sent from the Mixed Reinforcement Camp, was like being wrapped in a hot, damp cloth.

Gilbert's Dogras also had transport waiting for them. He left for his unknown destination complaining of prickly heat, and no doubt working out a suitable combination of leaves, powders or drops to cope with it in the long-term. We would miss Gilbert and his idiosyncracies.

The Reinforcement Camp had been set up among the palms of a surburban park. Thatched huts with walls of woven palm fronds lay back from the well-rolled soccer and hockey pitches which served as a parade ground. They housed a variety of units and servicemen of many nationalities. Most were Indian, but there were quite a number of Free French and Dutch. The occupants of the officers' quarters and Mess were similarly cosmopolitan.

Transit camps are soul-destroying places to be stranded in for any length of time. According to Ceylon Army Command, we'd be there about ten days, though fortunately most of the Sappers could be usefully employed. It was a curious situation to be in charge of a Company subject to orders by the Camp Commandant as well as by CAC Staff Officers.

Major Collis, the Commandant, with storm damage to be repaired, leapt at the arrival of an Engineer Company, so squads were soon busy in and about the Camp, and CAC also wanted detachments to help with a variety of jobs. It was better than having to find trivial tasks for skilled craftsmen, but the main difficulty was keeping track of them. The Subedar was particularly concerned about allowing them too much freedom in the big city, beyond his immediate control. We'd drawn up a code for local leaves out, but could do little about the dispersed working parties.

The whole camp had an "Alice Through the Looking Glass" atmosphere. Collis himself was something of an eccentric. A corpulent stockbroker, somewhat short on "gees" and "aitches", he'd already spent more than two years looking after these transient communities. He had a wine-bar approach to everyone and everything.

''Ow your bearded wonders settlin' in then?' was his greeting when I called on him on Tuesday morning. His comments were usually kind, though not always. He seemed to have an unshakeable dislike of the French.

On Wednesday an order was posted naming Box as Duty Officer for the coming Friday. With only two of us to cope with the working parties, and having just heard that we'd be embarking the following Wednesday, I buttoned-holed Collis and suggested he leave Box off the list.

'Absolutely right, old chap. Should 'ave thought of it. No use floggin' things. My fault, forgot you was short-handed. Trouble is these bleedin' Frogs. If you detail 'em and they don't feel like it, they bloody well pretend they can't read English! Orders are supposed to be translated anyway; but Captain Boussac's as slippery as French polish!' He warmed to his theme. 'Every Friday they're orf like the clappers to Mountbatten's French-struck Wrens up at Trinco. Due back Sunday night, most of 'em turn up on Tuesday! They been 'ere six weeks waitin' for postin's. Even when they're in Camp they sod about . . . collectin' fireflies and stuffin' 'em under mosquito nets! *Up* de Gaulle, as yer might say!'

However he was helpful in providing the odd truck and driver, which meant we could keep an eye on the outside work. CAC had asked us to meant we could keep an eye on the outside work. CAC had asked us to repair the slipways used by small motorised fishing boats along a creek ten miles south of the city, and on the Thursday Jemadar Mangal Singh had half his Platoon working there. During the afternoon I drove out to see them . . . a visit which was to add one more name to the Company strength!

The Jemadar led the way across the beach, walking into a gusty breeze which brought the breakers crashing and bubbling over the rocky outcrops along the shore, past lines of men hauling on ropes, heaving in their catch against the resistance of shelving sand and creaming surf. We continued along the bay to where the Sappers were working on a slipway running down to a palm-fringed creek. A number of the colourful boats which carried out the nets were beached high up among the vivid green shrubs.

One of the welders brushed past us, carrying water in a mess-tin to a small furry object the size of a brick, lying panting under the keel of a boat. Tongue lolling out, head and flanks heaving, the tiny brown puppy hardly had the energy to stand and sip the water. It had a sharp, alert face and the pointed ears of a young jackal. They'd teased and chased it almost to exhaustion, but its eyes were lively enough.

After chatting for a while, I left them to it and drove back through the city to confirm Wednesday's arrangements. By the time I'd returned to the Camp, Box was back. He'd been to see if a *mochi* could make him an outsize pair of chaplis. As I described the visit to Mangal Singh, I sensed he was waiting to tell me something. When I'd finished, he pushed open the bathroom door and pointed to a small brown puppy, attached to the handle of the outside door by a rough coir rope. He stretched down and ruffled its ears.

'Someone in 3 Platoon brought him back in one of the trucks. They don't particularly want to keep it, and in any case the Jemadar won't have it in the huts. I'm going to see if I can find someone in the Mess to take care of him.'

Next morning, after feeding it, cleaning up after it, and taking it to and from the Mess, where no one wanted it, Box was getting quite possessive about the small furry object. As we walked over to the Mess in the evening, he confessed that he'd instructed Sanichar Singh, our First Grade Carpenter, to make it a kennel.

By the following morning it had acquired the name "Furry", had a smart collar and a rifle-sling lead, and Prem Singh had written him in on the Company strength. Two days later he had a desirable residence with "FURRY" painted on the roof in black letters, and from then on travelled as part of the establishment, getting plumper, though not much larger, and developing an upright head-tilted-back posture from gazing up to see where Box's voice was coming from.

On Monday we called-in the working parties and decreed Tuesday a day of rest and repairs, to prepare for embarkation the following day. Inevitably a small, perplexing problem emerged, involving yet again Pritap Singh's underlings in the Stores. With two hundred Sikhs on the strength, most of them already showing their worth, by now Bachan Singh should have receded into gratifying obscurity. Yet here he was once more at the heart of the issue. Surprisingly, however, it was the earnest, hitherto dependable Joginder Singh who presented the real problem.

Most of the Camp surroundings was out-of-bounds, except for a small local bazaar, which was a bustling, noisy attraction for off-duty troops. Here, among the gaudily decorated open-fronted shops, the flimsy stalls, and the perambulating street hawkers, was a concentration of interpreters of horoscopes and fortune-tellers. The judgements of such men are widely respected throughout the city, though presumably their status varies subjectively! It was here in the bazaar that Bachan Singh had received the prediction he most wanted to hear. Military prowess awaited him . . . promotion would follow promotion! Excitedly, he'd passed it all on to his fellow Stores Sapper, Joginder Singh, and together they'd hurried back to the bazaar and sought out the same seer.

Unfortunately, for his small payment Joginder Singh had received a much less propitious forecast . . . ominous in fact. On their return, he'd gone straight to Pritap Singh; and an hour later the Jemadar informed Box that one of his Sappers was refusing to cross water, for reasons he, Joginder Singh, would not divulge.

Threats of summary justice and official charges had brought no response, and since late afternoon Joginder Singh had been sitting on his charpoy. The Subedar had finally played his trump card and sent for the Religious Teacher; though as I walked across the parade ground discussing the matter with Pritap Singh I didn't know this. However, there in front of us was an unmistakable white-bearded figure, making his way to the hut concerned. As Gurdev Singh strode purposefully into the billet, I thought we should wait . . . an appropriate text, gently explained would probably do the trick.

'About tomorrow, Jemadar . . .' was as far as I got. There was a resonant, outraged roar . . . a sudden crash . . . an ear-splitting shriek . . . a succession of dull thumps . . . and a eerie silence . . . before a dishevelled Joginder Singh emerged, his boots in his hand. I hastily turned away towards our quarters, but glanced back to see a composed Religious Teacher walking slowly through the palms towards the VCO's Mess.

'No, Sahib,' said the Subedar, later that evening. 'Joginder Singh is no longer raising any objections to travelling with us.'

CHAPTER SEVEN

So We've Arrived . . .

The Injian Ocean sets an' smiles,
So sof', so bright, so bloomin' blue;
There arn't a wave for miles and miles,
Excep' the jiggle of the screw.
Rudyard Kipling: *For to Admire* (1894)

We arrived at the docks at noon, and there she was . . . our transport to the distant atoll, gangways down, nets suspended from her gantries hanging loose on the quayside, small wavelets slapping at her sides. SS *Rajah* was a Heavy-Lift Ship, the largest of the line of cargo vessels berthed on the south side of the harbour.

A Liberty ship was edging in past the breakwater, tugs fussing about the northern end of the harbour, and a rusty-looking collier moving out from the Coaling Depot; but for the moment the southern end was a haven of calm. Scents of tea, spices, and tangy coir from the open-fronted warehouses mingled with the heavier dock-side smells of oil and tarry rope; an exotic hint, perhaps, of what might lie at the end of the journey . . . a palm-fringed island paradise? Of course, it wouldn't turn out like that . . . though perhaps it did.

Embarkation was straightforward enough, the only casualty my long tin trunk, full of clothing, personal possessions, and an extra illicit revolver . . . which would have its part to play. It'd slipped gently out of the rope cradle, hit the dock with a sharp metallic crack and, fortunately, bounded back onto dry land, split at one corner. It had then been pushed to one side, and obviously needed roping. As I scurried down the aft gangway with the two orderlies to collect the trunk, we were swamped by a tide of Dogras, struggling up with their kitbags . . .

66

and there on the quay, looking hot and harassed, was Gilbert Fouldes.

He'd arrived at his Infantry Batallion to find, as anticipated, that Ceylon Army Command had earmarked his Dogras to provide military support for a construction project; only it wasn't in Ceylon. So here he was, with an enlarged detachment, still on his way to an unknown destination, expecting to receive orders on arrival from a NOIC – the Naval Officer i/c Kulu Atoll . . . HMS *Taltara*.

The trunk recovered and Teacher Gurdev Singh once more delivered to a rigged-up shelter in the prow, we hung over the side watching the mounds of stores and supplies for the island being swung up-and-over our heads and down into the holds. A broad ramp had been let down to the quay amidships, and in front of it dockhands were arranging metal barriers. Fifty yards away, a huddle of small lean men in green turbans, carrying sticks, had gathered at a door set in the side of the huge metal dock-gate.

The door suddenly swung open and through it poured a stream of multi-coloured goats – brown ones, black ones, brown and white ones, black and white ones, brown and black ones – dozens of them, kept on the move by shouting, stick-waving and gate-banging. Between the barrier they poured, up the ramp, and into the ship itself. Soon after the hubbub had died down a string of bullock carts creaked up to the ramp, and crate after crate of chicken followed the goats aboard.

It was a splendidly mixed cargo. Overhead the cranes were swinging-in bundles of pipes and huge curved metal plates . . . possibly for oil tanks? Small combustion engines strapped to wooden frames were being shackled-up on the dockside. It all pointed to real work at last!

Gilbert was not sharing our cabin, but John Gossard was. He turned out to be the new Garrison Engineer, a last-minute replacement for the atoll's former GE, who'd already left for southern India. He had the battered look of my boyhood hero – Jack Dempsey. I was beginning to feel dwarfed, what with Box towering over everyone, Gilbert nearly six-foot, and now John Gossard, wearing a loose bush-jacket which made him look even bulkier than he was. His boxer's nose was no coincidence: during his first few years in constructional engineering on Clydeside he'd helped a curate friend with a boy's club in the Gorbals, and together they'd slugged it out with promising young fighters.

All this came out later. He knew no more about *Taltara* than we did;

67

though in due course the islanders would have cause to be grateful for his physical strength. Meanwhile he was simply a quiet, helpful cabin companion.

As we moved through the breakwaters and turned southward the ship scarcely rose or fell in a smooth, silky sea. Flying-fish skimmed and splashed back, clearly visible as they raced beneath the surface and skimmed again. There was no indication of the recent storms.

By midday Thursday, however, the wind was stronger and the ship was rolling, though even Gilbert seemed stable enough. We changed course a great deal, presumably for tactical reasons, and as night fell hove-to for a while in a silvery bowl, the waning moon not yet up. The heavens were three-dimensional. I was used to recognising the clusters of bright stars, but had never before felt them hanging over us.

Before dawn we were moving again, and at about ten o'clock HMS *Taltara* – more properly Kulu Atoll – came in sight, low on the horizon. We were relatively close-in, for the atoll averages only four feet above sea-level . . . a heart-shaped ring of coral islands, green with palms, enclosing a deep inner lagoon, some seven miles across.

We nosed into this inner harbour through a deep-water channel to the south of the atoll and, turning westward, approached the largest of the islands. Before us an unusual cargo vessel lay close-in parallel with the shore, almost touching a long wooden jetty. Beyond, the glare from the coral silhouetted Lowry-like figures on a busy dockside dominated by a two-storied balconied building, the Naval HQ. Along the shore in each direction small huts clustered amid the coconut palms.

With bells signalling and orders flying back and forth, we slid in almost alongside the cargo ship and dropped anchor. There was something odd about the way the vessel was lying. The name *British Sceptre* was reassuring enough, but we had the impression she'd been hit, and a closer look showed damage amidships. But there were other things to think about. Landing craft were ploughing towards us, accompanied by a number of smaller vessels. An hour later, the last of HQ Platoon, with Furry sitting like a mascot on the Company clock, had joined the rest of us on the shore.

The moment we'd disembarked one of the Docks Operating Company, a chunky little Lieutenant answering to "Smivvy", tackled Box about the equipment. At last, I thought, real organisation! We were taking over from a somewhat smaller unit and, again to my relief, Duncan Cooper, the O.C., was there to greet us. I'd seen his name on Orders but had never met him. His small detachment had already fallen out among the palms and there were noisy reunions with some of our Sikhs. Cooper had the lined, sallow look of someone who'd spent a long time in the humid tropics. With his floppy service hat on the back of his head he seemed very casual . . . not just casual, but abstracted. He was obviously involved in last-minute farewells and gave the impression he was glad to be leaving. It seemed as though SS *Rajah* was making a quick turn-round.

We'd expected to have some time with him, but to my surprise he put his hand on my shoulder and said, 'I've jotted down a few notes for you and there are some maps you'll find useful. I've already handed a bundle of files to your Subedar which you may, or may not want to hang onto.' Which seemed an odd introduction to what I'd been led to assume was a major engineering project. Before I could comment he'd spun round, making signals to someone by the jetty.

'Excuse me,' he said, dashing off towards a fair haired, florid-looking Captain, who was directing the loading and unloading with nasal tones and a vocabulary which suggested Paddington, Sydney rather than Paddington, W2. They disappeared behind a huge stack of crates. After several minutes Cooper reappeared and put his hand on my shoulder again, an irritating gesture. 'Sorry about that,' he said, still looking at the pile of crates. 'Had to stop Ozzie putting my shells in with the deck cargo . . . bloody dangerous!' . . . It sounded it!

'Would it be a good move to show us exactly where we're billeted?' I said. 'I can bring my Subedar with me.'

'Not really time I'm afraid, we're just waiting to shift our stuff . . . But that's where the Company lives,' pointing vaguely across the island to the left of the HQ building. 'Look this is roughly the lay-out.' He pulled out a pencil and drew an outline in the gritty dust covering the concrete hard. 'That's where you are . . . For the last week or two we've been building some extra accommodation for you. Just as well,' he added cryptically, 'we needed something to do. Tim Osborne, the GE, should have seen you in; but he was posted to Bangalore. They flew him out last week. I gather you've brought his replacement . . . which is he?'

I couldn't see John Gossard anywhere; but then he knew no more than we did.

'Should we run through the actual work you've got on hand?' I suggested, feeling he'd be off before I was even minimally in the picture. 'I imagine you've been up to your ears. Which is why . . .'

69

'Look,' he interrupted, 'there'll be a meeting shortly with the NOIC and your new GE. I suggest your 2 i/c stays with the Company until you've got your instructions.'

As he was speaking, a rather smooth Fleet Air Arm officer tapped him on the shoulder and murmured, 'Turner's waiting.' Cooper hastily introduced him as "Wings", which didn't help much . . . Nor were the introductions in the NOIC's cool shuttered office particularly helpful, for it was difficult to distinguish those who were leaving from those who'd be our colleagues on HMS *Taltara*. I recognised Ozzie, who seemed to be Beachmaster, though every minute or so someone whispered something to him and he responded with 'Stone the bloody crows!' and rushed out, finally disappearing altogether.

Captain Robert Turner, RN, shirt-sleeve smart, in contrast to the motley military assembly, presided with few words, but followed the clipped discourse from his Number One with a continuous attentive nod. Once again I'm afraid, with the judgement of youth, I viewed him as very elderly indeed. In this case he was, even by wartime standards, being semi-retired at Dartmouth when War broke out. Nevertheless, as Naval Officer Commanding a remote atoll, stiff with extravagant characters prone to irrational behaviour, we'd find that he seldom got things wrong.

All I can really remember is collecting a sheaf of instructions, scribbling down names and times, and trying to decipher it all during the afternoon. By which time the unforthcoming Cooper and his men had embarked. It seemed ludicrous that he'd been whisked away before he could elaborate on the work he'd been doing or, apparently, not doing. Yet there seemed no immediate problems. So, with the help of Ozzie and the Transport Pool, 725 began ferrying equipment along narrow palm-fringed tracks, across a wide coral runway, to the cluster of low thatched huts facing the distant sparkle of surf over the outer reef . . . home for the next eight months.

It had been a curiously inconclusive arrival. But I felt sure that tomorrow we'd get a clearer idea of the tasks facing our carefully assembled craftsmen.

CHAPTER EIGHT

Peculiar Priorities

All expectation has something of torment.
Benjamin Whichcote: *Moral Aphorisms* (1753)

Kulu Atoll lies within a degree of the Equator, an almost insignificant speck in the great expanse of the Indian Ocean. We'd landed on Manu, the largest of the islands, some two miles long and a half-mile across, close to where a narrow coral shelf supported the main jetty, serving the deep inner lagoon.

The outer, western side of the island was less developed, for here the palms fringe a storm-beach of coral debris some six feet above the sea . . . the atoll's highest natural feature. Beyond it a wide coral reef extends towards the open ocean, whose waves crash onto its outer edge with a continuous thundering roar, so much a part of the environment that you have to concentrate to hear it. This broken edge overhangs the sea-mount which supports the whole coral atoll, allowing a sheer drop beneath the blue waters . . . a thousand fathoms and more . . . to the bed of the Indian Ocean.

At low-tide the branching corals of this wide outer reef are partly exposed. Here polyp colonies create a variety of contrasting forms and colours . . . coral fingers, coral mushrooms, convoluted brain corals, and delicate calcareous fans. Among them live the shelly molluscs – the cowries, mitres, volutes and cones – along with more mobile inhabitants like the spiny lobsters and stripey sea-snakes. In due course, like Donald Cooper, we'd be concerned about safe transport for our own collections of shells! And in time would relish the fact that the clearer waters of the inner lagoon teem with fish of astonishing variety . . . small and shiny, flat and stripey, bulbous and spotted, and a few of threatening appearance like the sharks and barracudas. Here, too, in early evening we'd watch the dolphins leap in mid-lagoon, at about the time the first flights of fruit-bats were leaving the palms, where by day they'd hung in lumpy clusters, high among the fronds.

The other islands are mostly longer and narrower than Manu, but all are habitable . . . for, providently, wherever a borehole is drilled the coral yields drinkable water.

Long before we'd arrived causeways and bridges had been built to link the western islands, serving outposts like the small RAF base, which maintained that excellent form of transport – a Sunderland flying-boat.

Around Manu itself a narrow coral road threaded its way among the fringe of palms. Elsewhere, rough tracks had developed between the various units and fanned out from the Naval HQ and the jetty. The island's flat coral surface, once a tangle of evergreen shrubs with occasional palms, now had a runway for small planes, notably to allow sorties by an old Walrus, which was Wings' responsibility . . . though our main link with the outside world was a weekly visit by a Catalina flying-boat from Ceylon.

Before the Services moved in, early in the War, each of the main islands supported a stable Maldivian community, making a living from the coconuts and the sea . . . colourful, enterprising people who traded copra and coir, dried fish and shells; and when the winds were right, crossed hundreds of miles of ocean to the markets of Male or Ceylon, navigating without a compass. Most of them now lived in villages on the eastern islands receiving supplies in part compensation for the disruption, though they frequently crossed the lagoon to profit from roof-thatching or providing limes and fish, and occasionally turtles. Fishing remained a necessity, and conch shells still boomed the width of the lagoon, sending messages between the islands and directing their boats.

By the time we arrived, the occupying force was well provided for, with a degree of comfort, for generators maintained a steady supply of energy for refrigerators, ice-making machinery, and a soda-water plant! There was a pool of transport serviced by a REME detachment, run, flamboyantly, by William Q. Forrest-Hill, a former racing driver, who'd not only competed at Brooklands but as "Quentin Hill" had occasionally appeared on-stage in London revues. The pick of his trucks were sufficiently souped-up to make the round-island races alarming, especially as they took place after dark!

It would have been surprising if the island were not well equipped, for the technical know-how of its garrison was considerable. There were exceptions, of course. Gilbert, now "serving" with the Garrison Company, hardly came into that category; nor did that redoubtable Gunner Captain "Rosy" Sinclair, who'd been commissioned during the First World War and had served in India since the 'twenties. He'd twice been "busted", but was still soldiering on . . . though that, as we shall see, is another story.

This remote ring of islands was to be our base for many months, but on that first day, before the Company moved to its billets on the western shore, there was much to be done. I'd returned to the jetty to find the stores still being checked and Ozzie still "stoning the crows", and discovered that the Subedar had taken an advanced party to allocate quarters and establish the Office. I decided to join him, leaving Box to follow with the rest of the Company.

By mid-afternoon working parties and stores were arriving by truck, and on the small parade ground amid the palms the VCOs were busily redistributing it all. One of the drivers seemed to be looking for someone and handed Jemadar Bir Singh a small note, which he brought over. It turned out to be a curious message from Box, which read: 'Livestock following. Check on compound. Will come soon as poss.'

What livestock? What compound? We'd examined almost everything – the thatched Platoon huts, the water-tanks, the Nissen-hut store, the most spacious Office, and the cooking area. I'd had a quick look at our small living quarters – little more than huts with palm-frond walls, and a tiny bathroom facing the beach. We'd discovered an empty chicken run and a small garden with a few tatty banana plants and a patch of sweet corn, but what did Box mean by "compound"?

We found out half-an-hour later, when the first of the goats came straggling along one of the paths from the runway, followed by about eighty others, encouraged by four Sappers from HQ Platoon. At the same time I spotted Box standing up in a truck as it flickered past the palms along the coast road. As he caught sight of us, it veered inland.

'Meat on the hoof!' he yelled. 'We've got to look after them! Help the chaps drive them in! Where's the compound?' and then, in some alarm, as the first half-dozen trotted briskly towards the huts, 'Head them off!'

It took a little while to find the enclosure where the goats were to be penned; but way back towards the airstrip, off one of the tracks among the trees, we discovered a fenced, trampled clearing. Goats had obviously lived there quite recently.

Box explained, 'The Beachmaster asked me to take them over as soon as they came ashore. Apparently one of our chores is to look after the meat ration and keep it in good condition.'

I suppose Cooper should have told us, but he hadn't. So what did they feed on? Where should they browse? It was another thing to bring up at the Meeting at Garrison HQ in the morning. For the time being the Subedar made Naik Mukand Singh responsible for them.

Back in the small hut, the dependable Karam Singh had already distributed the few things I'd unpacked, and draped the mosquito-net over four upright canes around the camp bed . . . a sensible precaution for, apart from the ubiquitous mosquitoes and cockroaches, indigenous insect life obviously abounded in the green undergrowth. As we'd gone round the lines, we'd seen that bedbugs infested crevices in the wooden charpoys they provided for us, and recognised the large metal charpoy-boiling vats stacked behind the Stores.

I commented to Karam Singh on the number of hard-bodied flying beetles zinging about the room and ricocheting off the walls, and off us. He looked at me as if astonished at my lack of understanding.

'It is not their fault,' he said, as though I'd accused the whirring insects of wilful attack. 'They are confused at being inside when they should be outside!'

He steered me into the washroom and pointed to a large long-legged translucent green spider standing in my canvas wash-basin and to two small brown scorpions in the tin bath.

'There are many like these in the Captain Sahib's room,' he said cheerfully, shaking the scorpions onto the sand outside the back door. He carefully coaxed the spider onto a brush before depositing it where he'd dropped the scorpions . . . only they'd vanished . . . back into the hut? I began to wonder about his attitude to taking life, and whether he had Jain tendencies.

We'd only been on the island a matter of hours, but there was already a feeling that after the high-pressure, high-profile, hype and hustle at the Depot we could be in for an almighty let-down. During the evening such misgivings were to be raised to the level of concern.

The Officers' Mess faced the inner lagoon, so once the Platoons were settled-in we zigzagged across the island in one of the 15-cwts and parked in a clearing among the palms. In the starry dark the steep-pitched, over-hanging thatched roof and its raised platform-floor combined to make the Mess appear larger than it was. A yellowish light shone through the fly-screen door.

We'd changed into bush-jackets and slacks for, even an hour after sunset, the temperature had hardly dropped and the air had a heavy, humid feel to it. I remember the sense of relief as we walked into the airy room, extending up to the roof itself. Two punkahs hanging from the rough cross-struts were briskly ticking round, shaking the closely-woven fronds of the looser wall-panels.

The Mess appeared empty, but had a comfortable informal feel to it. There was a variety of light bamboo and cane furniture, with padded seats and cushions, obviously acquired from MT sources. On the bar, to the left of the door, a number of used glasses surrounded a bakelite-encased radio. The bar itself had a curved front of vertical bamboos and behind it two well-stocked shelves. A large gaudy advertisement, apparently acquired from a Colombo bottle-shop, hung from a nail on the lower shelf:

Scots Stag Whisxy for Happynes.
To specification of Jayaswamy Ranatunga

It had a line-drawing of a Scottish Highland scene resembling the Himalayas, with an ornate inset of a cow-like creature with two long straight horns . . . On closer inspection, most of the decorative bottles were empty.

Someone was moving about in one of the small alcoves at the end of the ante-room, otherwise the place seemed deserted. We were about to investigate the screened-off dining room to the right of the main Mess when a harassed-looking figure, boyish in a check shirt and light-grey trousers, appeared from the right-hand recess. 'Oh . . . hullo,' he said tentatively. 'I'm Ian Ashwell, Mess Secretary.'

We introduced ourselves, and gathered that he was one of three Gunner officers in the Mess. 'It seems rather quiet,' said Box.

'It's quiet at the moment, thank God!' he said, with some relief. 'The Dockies are still on duty with the lift-ship, and there's a party going on in the Ward Room. It usually happens when there's a vessel in.' He waved a hand around the ante-room. 'There was fearful thrash here last night. Rosy Sinclair insisted on finishing up most of the stock when he heard replacements were arriving. This is the first lift-ship for four months! We're almost out of whisky and beer, but he's placed an order for a six-month stock-up through the Naval Supply Officer, who indents for the whole atoll . . . Of course, you haven't met Rosy, our most ancient regular! He's not here tonight, he's gone to drool over the consignment. They won't release bottles 'til tomorrow, but he wants to be near them! He'll probably spend most of the night in the Wardroom anyway.'

'You get a choice of drinks?' asked Box, thinking, like myself, of the customary "take-it-or-leave-it" we'd been used to.

'Rosy and the NSO seem able to get a fair selection between them. The Navy's always stocked up with gin, and Rosy, saying unprintable things about Canadian Club, has put in for both Scotch and Irish this time . . . nothing like trying! Duty free, tuppence a nip, and nothing else to spend it on; you might as well drink the best, if you can get it!' He seemed to have cheered up.

'What about Mess dress?' I asked, looking at his bright red check.

'Informal, except on special nights and, of course, on visits to the Wardroom, or you can simply wear what you've got on. You'll need to keep your sleeves down after sunset – you've probably found out that what doesn't sting, bites!'

'What about the rest of the day?'

'Most of us wear working clobber or shorts. The whole place is free and easy . . . Look, if you're going through for a meal, I'll join you . . . hang on a minute.' He went into the other small room, then put his head out. 'I've just been clearing up in here after last night's havoc. This is the Information Room – one of the NOIC's bright ideas – supposed to keep us up-to-date!'

We followed him into the rather stuffy little room and watched him pinning a large, stained map of Euro-Asia onto a soft-board panel. A jumble of rubbish was piled onto two card tables.

'Can't find the pins or flags,' he said, pulling an ash-tray full of coral sand and cigarette stubs from under a torn pair of khaki shorts, draped across some of the rubbish. 'We generally mark up the War Zones and Fronts. There's supposed to be a Pacific Theatre map over there,' indicating a second, smaller soft-board. 'God knows where that's gone! The official Card-Room's over on the right, by the way, but this serves much the same purpose . . . I suppose I'd better pin back Smivvy's artwork.'

Smivvy's artwork proved to be a large Press photo of His Majesty presenting a medal to an RAF officer, to which Smivvy had added a balloon with spidery printing inside . . . 'How many F-Fokkers have you shot down then?' . . . I imagined it wasn't the sort of information the good Captain had in mind!

'Smivvy, Bob Smith . . . our tame Cockney . . . he's with the Dock Operating Company . . . a great chap . . . gets somewhat rough in his cups, but brightens the place up a bit.'

As we turned to the dining room, several trucks crunched-up outside. 'That sounds like Philip . . . the boss,' said Ashwell, pushing open the door for his Gunner Major, Philip Shuttleworth, who was ushering in John Gossard and Jim Welland, a young Geordie, in the Service Corps, closely followed by Gilbert and his O.C., Mike Robinson, a pleasant middle-aged Captain we'd met briefly by the jetty . . . There was an up-ending of bottles to discover any surviving contents.

'There aren't any chittis left after last night . . . just sign on the sheet,' said Ashwell, flapping about, and being entirely ignored . . . 'I think I'll go and eat,' he said, making for the screens.

The dining room was strictly functional, with folding chairs leaning against three cloth-covered trestle tables. Hearing someone arrive, a head peered over the screen at the far end, turned, and bellowed, '*Khana!*'; evoking a muffled response, presumably from the cookhouse beyond.

True to form, Gilbert drew attention to the small bottles of Vitamin C on the table. 'There's not much in the way of fresh fruit or veg,' said Jim Welland. 'You'll find a few limes and paw-paws about some of the old huts, but we always issue Vitamin C. Occasionally we get limes from the Maldivians. They collect them from an island twenty miles or so to the north.'

'Means they cross the Equator,' said Robinson.

Box informed the old stagers, with some pride, that we'd been told to bring plants and seeds with us, and were hoping to grow spinach, tomatoes, and marrows . . . a remark he later regretted. There was a suspicion of a smirk, but no one actually said anything until he'd finished. 'John Parsons would be interested in that!' commented Jim Welland, but didn't elaborate.

* * *

One of the first things we were to do was to appoint a Company Gardener, Lance-Naik Kirpal Singh. In no time he had the patch of sweet corn and straggly bananas cleared and planted. Soon the spinach, tomatoes, and marrows, thriving in the heat and humidity, were up and spreading. They continued to spread, in all directions! The largest marrow we had was the size of a thumbnail; the tomatoes, like yellow grapes, became rock-hard; but the spinach showed every sign of succulent growth. We all watched it with anticipation . . . and so did innumerable insects and molluscs; they stripped it bare!

* * *

Over the prunes the conversation turned to the fate of the *British Sceptre* and the future of its Master. According to Shuttleworth, one Sunday morning about five months ago, this semi-oil tanker, with oil-storage aft and general cargo for'ard, dropped anchor off the jetty, opposite the pipelines serving the island's inadequate storage tanks. About lunch-time, when fortunately many of the crew were ashore, a violent explosion hurled a mass of metal up and over the ship, peppering Naval HQ.

A Japanese two-man sub had come between the southernmost islands and aimed its small torpedo at the *British Sceptre*. It was almost too accurate, for it struck the vessel amidship without detonating its oil cargo, and only just below the waterline, where the inflow could be stemmed. Three injured lascars were brought ashore, but it had been a remarkable escape, not only for those aboard, but also for the Naval Headquarters. The Sunderland flying-boat was not at base, so Wings had taken his old Walrus over a broad sweep of ocean, but found no trace of the mother-ship.

The *Sceptre* had continued to list, so a month later a team of divers from Ceylon had helped the Navy secure it in its present position. There was considerable damage amidship, so that scaffolding, ladders and improvised cat-walks now connected the almost unscathed bridge with the more battered parts.

Almost at once CAC had decided that its oil-tank would give the island the storage capacity it needed and that another container was unnecessary . . . I looked at Box, and could see that he'd had the same immediate reaction. Why, then, had we been sent here? Why the urgent despatch of such a potentially efficient unit? There was a growing feeling that somewhere, somehow, wires had got crossed.

The *Sceptre's* new role had not pleased the heavily-bearded Norwegian Master, Bjorn Johannsen, who'd taken the sequence of events as a series of insults, first from the Japs and then from the planners of Ceylon Army Command. He'd retreated to his cabin and would have nothing to do with the dispersal of most of his crew, nor with social invitations from the NOIC, though he'd supervised the intake from two American tankers and continued to look after the needs of his skeleton crew . . . but that was all. It was rumoured that his replacement had arrived on the *Rajah*, though in fact he had not. So, for the whole of the time we were there, Johannsen continued his recluse-like routine, looking after his cage-birds and tending the tropical garden he'd established in the greenhouse atmosphere of the bridge.

We listened to Philip Shuttleworth's account with interest, though his curiously flat intonation made most things seem humdrum, even a disaster such as this. The others were more graphic. 'Missed all the excitement!' said Peter Bryant, who'd followed us into the dining room. Known as "Benjy" for some reason, he was in charge of the Artisan Works Company. 'By the time I got back from Havadu, everyone was beavering about the jetty, or getting the old Walrus airborne. Not what you'd expect on a civilised island on a Sunday. Ruined a good lunch-time piss-up in the Mess!' he moaned. He'd been on the atoll longer than anyone, claiming they'd forgotten where he was, and had a fairly sardonic approach to most things.

'It didn't ruin my afternoon,' chipped in Jim Welland. 'We were out in a boat recruiting a Maldivian work-party for the Monday. All I heard was a bang, about five miles away. "That's it," I thought, "someone's shot Rosy at last!"' . . . We wondered about Rosy.

CHAPTER NINE

. . . and a Goatherd

To travel hopefully is a better thing than to arrive,
and the true success is to labour.
R. L. Stevenson: *Virginibus Pueresque* (1885)

The following day we knew for certain that the decision to use the *British Sceptre's* tanks and abandon the proposed storage construction was made months ago, long before we'd set off . . . so why the urgent formation of such a streamlined unit?

The first assignments, through John Gossard, as Garrison Engineer, were unexciting, to put it mildly! It hardly needed a high-powered Engineer Company to extend Garrison Company's accommodation. It was true that another, larger, party was to build a second jetty for the RAF on Havadu, but there was no indication of any major project in the offing; and considering that there was an Artisan Works detachment on the island as well, how were we going to keep all our craftsmen employed? Wresting them from other active units now smacked of overkill!

As we walked back from the Meeting, temporary tenants of this sunlit green and blue and white world, our feelings were again ambivalent: interested and curious about this unusual, remote location, yet deflated by the apparent lack of purpose.

The Subedar took it all calmly. He'd obviously made the same appreciation and had drawn-up the Work and Parade State with Prem Singh, listing the duties for the day. We looked at it to see who'd not be available for the two work parties, and found a surprising number seemed to be occupied already. There were MT Drivers, Company Lines Guard, Guard for Garrison HQ, Guard on the Water-Tank, a party on

Water Supply, an Anti-Malarial party, Cookhouse Duties, Office Duties, Bootmakers, Tailors, Sweepers, a Gardener, a Hen Keeper . . . and a Goatherd.

'We have to send an anti-malarial party to spray any static water and areas of wet bush,' observed Bulwant Singh, seeing me sizing-up the list, 'and we share Garrison Guard duties with other units.'

'I was interested in the Hen Keeper,' I replied, squinting across the coral glare to the wired-in chicken run, where our newly acquired flock was pecking about, and with typical perversity pulling at fallen fronds through the mesh. I wondered if their welfare justified a full-time specialist.

'The Hen Keeper, Sahib, is Sapper Daya Singh. He will be responsible for the eggs, for selecting birds to kill, and for the repair and security of the hen-house, and must account to Jemadar Pritap Singh for all he does.'

'Oh well, that sounds as though he's going to be pretty busy!'

I immediately regretted sounding sarcastic, but the Subedar beamed his broadest.

'He will also act as a messenger and do duties for the VCOs.'

'What about the Goatherd? . . . Oh, by the way, I enquired and found that the goats can browse almost anywhere. The best places are the edges of the airstrip and any of the rough vegetation; but not near the coast road, and out of the unit areas, of course.'

'I have made a permanent appointment to Goatherd,' he replied. 'You will remember how Bachan Singh caught the egg-thief, and have seen how well he understands animals. I think he will do very well looking after the goats.'

This seemed to solve a number of problems. I agreed wholeheartedly, conscious of the fact that the Subedar had still made no mention of any relationship between them, and also began to reassess and rationalise it all. Perhaps, with so many tasks to keep them occupied, and doubtless more to come when we'd settled in, we could tick-over very comfortably, provided we found jobs for, say, two or three working parties of thirty or forty.

Then it dawned on me that we'd only been on the island a day, and here I was, feeling relieved that we could find ways of keeping them employed, whereas I'd been worrying all this time whether or not we had enough skilled men to cope! . . . The atoll was already slowing us down to its own pace!

I wanted to have a word with Box about the jetty construction, but he'd just left the Stores, where he'd been helping Pritap Singh. Through the palms I could see Box's angular bearer, Ajit Singh, walking Furry along the coast road. Failing to attract his attention, I set off after them. He'd stopped for a moment as Furry strained forward, confronted by a foot-long lizard, head angrily raked back to show its pulsating red and blue dewlap. The lizard ran back a yard up the road, stopped again, then scuttled into the bush. Ajit Singh began to walk the dog towards it.

'Where's the Captain Sahib?' I shouted. He pointed towards the sea, as Furry began tugging him along. It was low-tide, and down by the shore Box in his jungle-green battledress was bending in conversation with a bronzed figure in torn shorts and gym shoes standing in the shallow water. I crunched over the coral fragments and was introduced to Bill Forrest-Hill . . . How this ex-racing driver, part-time actor, turned REME officer had previously fitted into combat units of the 14th Army I can't imagine, but the demands of Ceylon Army Command and life on the atoll seemed geared for him. He was clutching a blue canvas bag and had spent the morning "shelling" on the wide outer reef. He splashed his way onto a ridge of firmer sand and tipped out the contents . . . a shiny tiger-cowrie, a heavy pink helmet shell, several file shells and a handful of wedges . . . and introduced us to what would become a compelling pastime. Within a day or two we were vying with the rest of them for the most comprehensive collection on the island.

'I bury them in a sieve,' he explained, 'let the ants clean 'em out; then wash them,' and described in some detail where in his opinion various species were most abundant.

'But it isn't just building a collection,' he proclaimed dramatically. 'What I love is the solitude, the wind, the sounds of the surf and the sea-birds.'

I recalled these sentiments, and his role as a part-time actor, a week later when, on the eve of Rosy's birthday, he was skidding his way between the palms during the first Grand Prix race since we'd arrived; and again later that night, when he was shouting for applause for his oft-repeated monologue about a merchant from Smyrna, a Sultan from Stamboul, and a very gullible young lady from Tiflis! Bill Forrest-Hill appreciated the sun-soaked solitude all the more when there was a pink gin and a receptive audience within reasonable distance.

Our second night on the island brought our first encounter with Rosy Sinclair, the third of the Gunners, though he seemed to have no working relationships with the other two whatsoever. It was not a felicitous meeting. He had just suffered a tragic loss . . . indeed we all had.

As soon as the Naval Supply Officer had, at last, begun to distribute the crates, Rosy was on the spot. The gin, always a Wardroom priority, was checked-in first; the brandies were accounted for; the beers were already stacked in the cool-house; but the whisky . . . no. Not a single case of whisky could be found. The Indent said, 'Whisky, Scotch' and, 'Whisky, Irish', but the Delivery Form said, 'Crème de Menthe' and crate upon crate bore the marking, 'Crème de Menthe'.

'Christ Almighty!' Rosy managed at last, visibly crumbling. 'Sticky Green!' . . .a six-month drought loomed ahead.

Rosy's first demotion from Captain, in the late twenties, had involved a three-day binge at Naini Tal, in the Himalayan foothills, when, among other things, he'd precipitated a boat-load of Memsahibs, staying with the Governor of the UP, into The Lake. His second, more spectacular descent, from Major, had occurred on the North-West Frontier shortly before the War, when he'd attempted to bombard the wrong target, but had been rescued from tragedy by his inept map-reading. During the last two years he'd been shunted from unit to unit and finally jettisoned in this inaccessible spot, as far from the Depot as possible.

Just before lunch, apparently, he'd rolled uninvited into the Wardroom and called for attention, his face turning purple. In a sweeping, all-embracing statement, his precise, clipped voice had accused the Navy of gross incompetence. They were used to him, but his oft-repeated demands to see the NOIC became boring, and his vivid descriptions of the Stores Officer as a "drunken doggie" and "incompetent sea-cook" became unbearable, so that eventually the OOD passed on a few home truths and had bundled him out.

When Box and I first saw him he was sitting by the bar in the Mess, directly below the radio, facing into the room, glass in hand, as though he were about to chair a meeting but hadn't the energy to call to order those unconcernedly reading old magazines, chatting, or swatting at the hard zinging beetles that became so frenzied at this time of evening.

Mostly he muttered, but occasionally raised his voice above the radio's static crackling and the lament of a distant, distressed Indian vocalist, shouting hoarsely, 'They can throw their stinkin' green noggin in the oggin!'

Ian Ashwell beckoned us, 'Don't get involved,' he warned. 'Take no notice. Walk past if you want a drink . . . there's beer on ice in the bucket behind, or grab a measure from the bar and help yourself from the bottle; the chittis are on the back shelf.'

I'd decided to dress informally and was wearing a white cricket shirt and khaki slacks. Rosy followed me with his eyes, seemingly without interest; but as I eased a couple of bottles from the bucket, a rasping voice behind me enquired: 'You in the white shirt! Yes, you! You in Naval Intelligence? Never seen you before! If you *had* any bloody intelligence you'd disguise yourself as the Redeemer and turn some of that green rot-gut into Scotch!'

I pretended not to hear and asked for a pencil to sign the chitti. Box stood up and started tapping the pockets of his bush-jacket. Rosy peered up at him. His thick voice took on an incredulous tone. 'Now what've we got? General bloody de Gaulle? Your lot might have got away through Dunkirk, but you'll never get away from this bloody atoll with this incompetent Naval mob in charge!'

He seemed to be recovering, but his eyes went out of focus again, and he sat staring into the room . . . Five minutes later, he stood straight up, gazed round in a benevolent manner and enquired in a quiet, level voice, 'Anyone comin' in for dinner?'

We went in for a meal about half-an-hour later and found him sitting next to John Gossard, apparently entertaining him with stories of action on the Frontier and accounts of scandalous *shikar* trips during his leaves in Kashmir.

'You would have thought he was as sober as a judge,' was John's assessment, 'and very amusing. Yet I'd watched him put back half a bottle of brandy after lunch, and he was still at it when I came back this evening.'

'That's just it,' said Bryant. 'It's the uncertainty which makes it so difficult. The Gunners really haven't any idea how to deal with it, or what to do with him. I don't think Phil, his O.C., understands what the matter is.'

'What is it then, apart from the tipple?' asked Box.

'It was bloody silly sending Rosy here, anyway . . . absolutely the worst place. He's got nothing to do and he's scared of the future. Most of us have a home background, someone to go back to when this rubbish is over, and a job to get on with; but Rosy's been a Mess bachelor all his life. Even if he stays in the East, things are going to be very different for him. "Quit India" isn't just a student protest any more . . . He gets on well enough with Ian most of the time, but he won't speak to Phil for days on end, except with the utmost formality.'

Michael Baxter, the Signals Captain, was less understanding. 'Of course he shouldn't have been sent here; but it's stupid to make excuses for him. He's a self-indulgent bastard! If he lets off like he did last week I'll have a crack at him!'

John Parsons nodded in agreement. He was also a Signaller, dark, aquiline and so closely resembling Baxter that they were usually known as the "Signals Twins", compulsive card-players, spending almost as much time in the Wardroom as they did in the Mess. They considered Rosy inconsiderate and provocative, so he took a particular delight in needling them, as we saw the following night, when another outburst might well have led to the threatened punch-up.

About an hour after dinner, Rosy walked into the tiny card-room during a vital hand of bridge, watery-eyed, and trying to peer at their cards. They were reasonably tolerant until he began bantering with his usual aggressive attempt at humour.

'I saw you kick his foot, Michael!'

'I'm not Michael.'

'I saw you kick his foot, John . . . or whatever your bloody name is.' He advanced a shaky pace and peered across the table. 'So that's why they call you the Signals Twins. I thought you might be more subtle . . . bit of ear-pulling or finger tappin' . . . you can read Morse, I suppose? Foot-kickin's a bit crude for a Signals expert!'

'Push off, Rosy!'

'Don't talk to me like that, Michael!'

'I'm not Michael.' He put his cards down and folded his arms.

'Who you are's irrelevant. It's what you're doin' we're discussing!'

'We're not *discussing* anything, Rosy. We're playing cards. Now go and get a drink and stop interfering.'

Rosy switched to a forced jocularity. 'You're standin' me a drink? Splendid!' He draped an imaginary napkin over his arm. 'I am a bloody efficient *khidmatgar*, and I shall bring you all the drinks you require, and I shall bloody well bring you the chitti to sign as well!'

And so it went on, until Baxter got Ian Ashwell to steer him into another argument by the bar . . . and after a few minutes he'd forgotten the bridge players.

The problem was to solve itself in the weeks ahead; but in the meantime Rosy came to pride himself on his "sticky green" concoctions.

He had it neat, on the rocks, with soda, with lime, and with dashes of almost everything else he could lay his hands on.

For the Sikhs, Sunday was a day of settling in, literally letting their hair down and making the most of the island's liberal supply of fresh water, obviously relieved at no longer being herded from place to place by train or ship.

After breakfast I wandered over to the lines. There was almost a holiday atmosphere, which reinforced the irrational, guilty feeling that we should all be involved in something more demanding. Some of them had collected hermit crabs from the lower branches of the trees along the shore and detached them from their borrowed accommodation. They were squatting in a semi-circle, watching the dispossessed crabs trying to tuck their soft-skinned abdomens into whorly mollusc shells and conical augers. There was a shout of laughter as one succeeded and the thin dappled cone began to wander about, uncertainly erect once more, and echoing shouts of applause from beyond the as-yet-undeveloped garden, where an open space had been sanded by Naik Mukand Singh, who lived for wrestling . . . For the moment, none of them wished for something more demanding.

We spent an hour or so with Prem Singh and the Subedar, examining miscellaneous files and equipment left behind by Cooper's detachment. There was a check-list among the papers he'd handed over which, to our surprise, included a small boat and a detachable outboard engine. It was apparently held by the Navy and kept somewhere on their hard, north of the jetty. With as little to do as the rest of them, it was worth seeing if we could find it and try it out.

We followed one of the rougher tracks across the island to the inner lagoon and found an Indian AB on duty on the hard. Yes, he knew the Sappers' boat. He obligingly found a couple of life-jackets, helped carry the light clinker-built dinghy from the shelter down a rather rickety ramp and attached the engine. The planking was in reasonable condition, and it appeared to have been in regular use.

We checked the fuel, and looked around in case we should notify someone of our departure, but there was hardly a soul about, apart from our Indian friend, who nodded approvingly as the engine fired.

We moved clear of the inner reef before chugging northward, a strong northerly breeze rustling the palms and whipping up choppy waves in the lagoon. With the sun virtually overhead sharp darts of light flickered from one wavelet to another. For the first time since we'd arrived I felt totally relaxed, the more so as neither Box nor I felt obliged to natter.

The tide was on the turn and we could feel the rush of water coming through the gap between Manu and Maladu islands, swirling round the piers of the long low bridge . . . an interesting construction, which couldn't have been easy to complete with that sort of scour . . . the kind of job I'd thought we'd be tackling.

Maladu appeared much less developed than Manu, with Maldivian huts beneath the palms and outriggers drawn-up on the beach; though whether these belonged to fishermen or were used to ferry the workforce across the lagoon we couldn't tell. Many of the locals helped to weave and fix the *kajjan*, the palm-frond thatching, on various buildings, and crossed the lagoon each day.

There appeared to be little activity at the RAF base on Havadu, where Box was due to help with the new jetty. He viewed the site from a distance as we ploughed our way up the western parts of the lagoon, keeping well clear of the inner reef.

The small boat bucketed about again in the choppy sea as we approached the tiny island of Funahera in the far north-west. Almost completely covered with dense green vegetation, its tall palm fringe was complete, except where a number of huts clustered about a concrete structure and half-a-dozen Indian troops were swilling through clothes on the shore.

We turned back, bouncing sufficiently for Box to keep wiping the spray from his glasses, and headed for Manu, the tide running even more strongly between the islands and carrying us some way into the lagoon. I suppose we should have checked on local hazards before we set out, but the whole island had seemed to lie in a midday torpor, reflecting what Benjy had felt about the disturbance of Sunday lunch-time by the Japanese!

It had been an enjoyable recce. Above all we'd gained an impression of space and an appreciation of scale. Out in the lagoon one saw the fragility of this ring of coral islands . . . nothing more than a broken crust, scarcely maintaining itself above the surface of the ocean.

Back in the Company lines Box was waylaid by Chega Singh, the duty clerk, but I continued along the shore, picking my way through the leafy trash beneath the palms, sunlight flickering over the fallen, yellowing fronds. Crabs sidled out of old, split, greying husks, making by instinct for the beach, and high overhead there were sharp cracking noises among the swaying clusters of green-cased nuts, some soft enough to attract the fruit-bats, the others potentially lethal from sixty feet up. A heavy thud, a few yards away, justified the warning we'd repeated in Company Orders.

Clear of the trees, I sat among the bushes, taking in the eddies and swirls of water as the waves crashed over the edge of the reef.

'We are far from England, Sahib, and from the Punjab.'

I'd been deep in thought and had no idea where Bulwant Singh had come from.

'Room for you here, Subedar Sahib; come and sit on the end.'

He lowered himself onto the old splintery palm trunk, half-hidden by bushes. In a white shirt and light blue baggy trousers he still looked, in his chunky way, as spruce as ever.

I told him about the trip, then asked how he felt about the Company's new home. He smiled, 'It is certainly unlike any posting I have had before. In any active Company there are always problems, though they differ from one Company to another.' He began to reminisce in his unhurried way.

'On the Frontier the problem was protecting ourselves, building *sangars*, guarding the work parties . . . Against the Italians we were always moving, there were transport problems . . . While in the jungle, as well you know, the worry is about supplies . . . though we learn to improvise. The problems we face are always changing.' I nodded, and let him go on.

'Here, of course, it will be different . . . keeping each man active, but preparing for the future. We are part of the force preparing to invade Malaya, who knows when we may move? . . . We must not forget our military training.'

'You're right, Subedar Sahib. It's important to keep everyone fully occupied, but I hope we can find suitable jobs for them.' Then, lightening it, 'Perhaps we should add "Fishermen" to our list, as well as "Henkeeper" and "Goatherd"!'

Bulwant Singh didn't say anything for a moment or two, then looked at me with his broadest of smiles and said, 'Yes, Sahib, our Goatherd is a good example. He is the right man for the job. You know, of course, that he is my brother's son.' . . . I felt a wave of relief.

'We are a military family and my nephew, Bachan Singh, is conscious of tradition. I meant what I said when you asked about him. He is most willing, but he is also awkward and has difficulties . . . To me he is

Sapper Bachan Singh, Company Goatherd. To my family he is Sapper Bachan Singh, as I was once Sapper Bulwant Singh, serving his country.'

This was the first of many quiet talks with Bulwant Singh. He considered his opinions and expressed them carefully. I have never met a more straightforward nor more compassionate man. He could philosophise about life in village India, standing well away from it all; but when he talked about his own village he spoke specifically about the comings and goings in that small part of rural Punjab where so many of his relatives farmed, and sometimes feuded. He had a firmness of principle where Sikh ways of life and traditions were concerned.

He also knew, before we left the island, that Partition was inevitable, and all that might mean for the people of the Punjab . . . and, months later, on our last night together, back on the Deccan, when I was honoured to accept from him the Sikh insignia, I handed him what, in all seriousness, he had requested . . . my "spare" revolver, with the numbers filed off.

As he walked away along the beach, I felt he'd chosen exactly the right moment to involve me in his family affairs. We could adjust to our somewhat unusual circumstances here on the atoll without any reserve . . . Wiggling the sharp coral sand out of my chaplis, I went back to tell Box.

CHAPTER TEN

Ailments Assorted

Good doctors do not like big bottles.
German Proverb

Looking back, our occupations seemed to become increasingly eccentric, though we'd settled into a familiar daily routine. An early morning *'Cha, Sahib!'* from Karam Singh . . . it was still dark. Into the tiny bathroom as the few remaining mosquitoes zinged away to their daytime retreats and the sharp cries of the seabirds heralded the instant dawn. Then on parade at 0630 in broad daylight, for here on the Equator the days leapt into action as swiftly as they faded into night. It was roll-call, spot inspections, and off on the various jobs.

The pattern was broken, however, on the morning after Rosy Sinclair's birthday. Celebrations in the Mess and our first experience of a 15-cwt round-the-island Grand Prix had been followed by a mad enquiry to find who'd come second to Bill Forrest-Hill, who invariably skidded in a bend or two ahead of the field. Mal Baird, Ozzie to all, had clearly and noisily arrived second, but Smivvy had objected on the grounds that he'd cut corners. Gilbert, rationing his drinks as conscientiously as his potions, had been deemed sober enough to adjudicate . . . lunatic entertainment, which had continued far into the night.

'Cha, Sahib.' As usual the startled lizards rustled about in the thatch. *'Achha, Karam Singh, mihrbani.'* I blearily pushed away the mosquito-netting, sipped at the tea, pottered gently into the small bathroom and switched on the yellowish light . . . something was scuffling about outside.

'You there, Martin?' called a strained, querulous voice.

'Who is it?' I looked out towards the beach . . . and there was Gilbert Fouldes, clutching his face and looking very rough indeed. Carefully abstemious, he couldn't have acquired a hangover from last night's mayhem.

'Come in . . . What's the matter?'

He walked round the hut and came into the light, still holding his cheek. 'I've been bitten by a scorpion, it was in my face flannel. I can't bend my neck . . . it's sore behind my ear . . . and Mike Robinson's not brought the truck back!'

'Take your hand away.' Scorpions? Fatal? Scorpions had worried us for days. We'd found them under the top of the office desk, and had got into the habit of flipping up the thunder-box lid before squatting.

'Karam Singh!' I yelled.

'*Ji, Sahib!*' He was just outside.

'Fetch the Captain Sahib!'

I could hear him telling Ajit Singh to wake up Box, who had no difficulty in switching from asleep to awake, and invariably got up after I did.

'Box, Gilbert's been bitten by a scorpion. Get Mehenga Singh to drive us to the Doc . . . take over Parade and tell the Subedar.'

Ten minutes later we were rushing across the airstrip, bound for the Naval cabins . . . "huts" to us, "cabins" to the Navy!

The MO, Doc Walsh, was up, beard trimmed and already looking efficiently smart.

'Shaw . . . this is a surprise! What can I do for you?'

'It's Gilbert, he's been bitten by a scorpion.'

'Yes . . . I've been . . . bidden . . . by a . . . schorbion.' Doc pulled Gilbert's hand out of the way and identified the point of attack.

'Right! Quick! No time to lose! Get this down!' He reached across for a half-bottle of Hennessey and glugged out nearly a tumbler-full.

'Brown scorpions have a nuisance value,' he said slowly. 'You'll have a bit of a headache and it may even close your eye for a while. But, not to worry, it will gradually go down. This,' tapping the bottle, 'is the only thing. It has absolutely no effect on the poison . . . none whatsoever . . . but it's a splendid anaesthetic, and if you want another after you get to the Mess, have it . . . and I'll bet you can't eat breakfast.'

As we turned to leave, he added, 'Interesting that the Chinese use the venom as a cure for facial paralysis! And in some parts they breed scorpions as a delicacy!'

'Ah!' said Gilbert.

He then had another, larger, but inferior brandy in the Mess, and had to endure detailed accounts of scorpion bites . . . on the bum, on the elbow, and behind the knee . . . but was obviously feeling sufficiently anaesthetised not to mind missing breakfast. By lunch-time the swelling had subsided sufficiently for him to talk freely, and become the fourth brown-scorpion bore in the Mess.

Two days later we called in Doc Walsh for a more serious incident. Strong southerly winds had persisted, but, despite Orders, two Sappers just off guard-duty chose to relax beneath an eighty-foot palm. Sapper Mohinder Singh had removed his pagri, but fortunately left his hair piled-up, which probably saved his life. The green, hard coconut split his skull.

By the time I'd been called back from Havadu, Doc had the unconscious Mohinder Singh in the Sick Bay. He'd realised at once that it would be touch-and-go if he had to deal with him in our small hospital unit, so by evening the Sunderland flying-boat was on its way to Colombo and base hospital, with Doc's understudy and the chief medical orderly looking after the stricken Sikh.

This was the last we saw of Mohinder Singh, for a year later he was discharged through the Depot, though the sequel was worthy of the eccentricity which characterised almost every phase of life on Kulu Atoll.

We'd set up a formal Court of Inquiry and Prem Singh had duly typed out the proceedings. I'd read them, signed them, and put them in my Out tray, and that was that . . . an unfortunate, unlucky accident, though he'd only himself to blame.

Six months later, the week before we were due to leave the atoll, Prem Singh put the same, now-wrinkled sheets of buff paper in my In tray . . . they had winged their way to Colombo, travelled to Delhi, worked their way up a pile of similar Forms, travelled back to Colombo and, brought over by Catalina, now sat once more on my desk . . . together with a cover note, which read:

'You have omitted to fill in para 9c (page 2) . . . "Was this due to enemy action?" . . . If YES give detail under 9d . . . You are requested to do so and return **immediately**.'

Box drafted the reply and I pencilled it in:

'The Japanese, fully aware of the unusual importance of Sapper Mohinder Singh to the Allied War Effort, with commendable cunning infiltrated agents disguised as monkeys, who, seizing the right moment when he was poorly protected, proceeded to hurl coconuts at the Sapper beneath, with an accuracy that must suggest long hours of specialised training, coupled, of course, with characteristic Japanese foresight.'

Prem Singh typed it and quite solemnly presented it for initialling, until I caught his eye! . . . It may have come back for further comment; but, if so, we never got it.

About this time Doc Walsh must have thought we were deliberately choosing a weird assortment of ailments to try out on him for, three weeks after the coconut incident, I had to approach him on behalf of one of our most talented craftsmen, Grade I Carpenter Sanichar Singh. The ailment had come to light partly though our growing obsession with shelling.

Every spare moment saw us out among the splendours of the coral shelf. Feet protected by gym shoes, we splashed about, knee-deep at the most, amid the colonies of corals. There, among their beautiful intricate branches, was a rough old world, where the occupants of helmet shells preyed on the sea-urchins, and those of the innocent-looking cone shells stabbed and poisoned their victims. There were abandoned shells a-plenty. It could be mildly hazardous, though the only person to be reduced to crutches by coral sores was Gilbert, who did as little shelling as anyone.

As we began to specialise, we needed somewhere to store the classified shells. Box came up with the sound idea of using Sanichar Singh's expertise to make a really good sandalwood show-case . . . a box with drawers of differing depth. We could even use it as a Trade Test to up-Grade other promising Carpenters, by getting them to make copies.

This sounded as though it might suit all concerned, so I sent for Sanichar Singh to sound him out, before putting the idea to the Subedar. There was a long delay . . . Finally, to my surprise, Bulwant Singh himself appeared. He walked smartly into the Office, but didn't come right up to the desk.

'You wish to see Sanichar Singh, Sahib?' He sounded a little tentative.

'Yes, I want him to make a small cabinet to be used as a copy for Trade Testing our other carpenters, a good incentive for them to get extra pay.'

'I'm afraid Sanichar Singh is sick and may not be able to help for several days.' He sounded uncharacteristically evasive. It was also rather odd, for I couldn't recall seeing Sanichar Singh's name on the Sick List.

'What's the matter with him, Subedar Sahib?' A direct question merited a direct reply. He didn't hesitate. 'Sanichar Singh is the finest carpenter in the whole Engineer Group, but I'm afraid he's been chewing opium. In Poona there is no problem, he spends his money always with the same supplier and can do his work to perfection, as you know. He chews little, but he can't do without it. In Colombo he could only buy a small supply, for they are charging him ten times what he gives to his friend in Poona . . . Now his supply is finished.'

'Why didn't you tell me before, Subedar Sahib?' It was not the right question, and he ignored it.

'Yesterday I found him shaking and not able to do his job. Tomorrow, Sahib, I would have had to send him to report sick and, of course, would have told you all I knew about it. But some were saying that he could get opium from another source on the island, and I wanted to investigate this carefully. I'm sure this is a false report. It's as well you now know the exact situation. He will report sick immediately.'

I walked over to 2 Platoon huts with the Subedar. The sun was slanting through the open window and a swaying palm flickered shadows across the sad figure lying on a grey blanket on his charpoy. He struggled to sit up and swung his legs over the side.

'He is not shaking, it's just the light,' Bulwant Singh pointed out, as if there was nothing else he could say. He wasn't shaking, but he looked at me with watery eyes, mouth sagging as though expecting me to strike him. I, too, could find nothing to say. In his mid-thirties, he was as fine a carpenter as you would come across, a steady amiable chap. I hoped we wouldn't have to return him to Depot, but also wondered what we were going to do with him . . . I got Doc Walsh to have a look at him.

'Let him carry on,' advised Doc. 'I'll give you a pellet and show you how to deal with it.'

'A pellet?'

'A small ball of opium. You can keep it in your safe. I'll show you how much to issue each week. He's been on this for years and seems quite good at controlling it. Letting him have a week's supply should be quite all right. I'll give you the medical bumf and a copy of my report, just to cover you.'

And so I deposited the sticky, blackish ball in the Company safe; and each Friday, *arzi* day, just to remind us, a soldierly Sanichar Singh would salute and carry away his week's supply.

He made me the sandalwood chest for my shells, so beautifully finished that after some fifty years of showing-them-off there is no play in any of the sliding trays. The other two cabinets are good, too, but not in the same class . . . though they served to raise Grade III Carpenters Tara Singh and Bola Singh to Grade II, and brought them a modest increase in pay.

CHAPTER ELEVEN

It's Far from Rosy

When wise men play the fool they do it thoroughly.
Italian Proverb

It was almost inevitable that in an enclosed environment like ours the more extravagant personalities, with time on their hands, would clash; and occasionally the island became noisy with controversy.

The jobs varied in interest, though few were any real challenge. The NOIC, for instance, had decided to extend the hard south of the jetty and put in a couple of slipways for small vessels – a straightforward task for 3 Platoon, which had been working on the slipways in Ceylon. So we briefed Jemadar Mangal Singh and he duly took two Sections along to Naval HQ . . . Shortly after they'd started, he sensibly suggested using our small motor-boat to ferry tools and materials to the work-site, and I'd agreed to let them use it, especially as Havildar Sohan Singh, used to assault river crossings, had volunteered to look after it. Motor-boats fascinate people, and Sohan Singh was no exception. I had misgivings when I saw him revving-up and doing great sweeps into the lagoon; so I left firm instructions about the use of the craft before I went off to see 2 Platoon.

When I returned, a couple of hours later, Bjorn Johannsen, Master of the *British Sceptre*, was leaning over the side with a megaphone in his hand. As the vessel rocked on the swell, shafts of reflected light swept up the side of the ship, briefly illuminating the Master's shaggy features and highlighting his great beard and his brow in a most sinister manner. He looked like a huge Kodiak bear.

He'd been watching me and gathered that I was connected with the working party on the hard, which as far as I could see was getting on with things in an orderly way.

'You are in charge?' he shouted tinnily through the megaphone.

I pointed to my chest in a "Who? . . . Me?" gesture.

'You are in charge?'

'Yes! This is my Company!' With the wind against me, I wasn't sure he could hear.

'Twice they have cut my cable! . . . You understand? . . . You are hearing?'

I heard, and looked down through the clear water over the inner reef, through the weaving patterns of tropical fish, but couldn't see anything unusual.

'Once I have sent a man to mend it. Now they have again cut it with their boat! I have said they must not cut my cable! . . . You understand?'

I thought it time to get hold of the Jemadar, but as I turned Johannsen began beating the megaphone on the side of the ship. 'When again they cut my cable the second time, I send my man to Captain Turner . . . You hear me?'

I still couldn't see any cable, taut or loose.

'You – will – not – cut – my – cable! I have no talk with shore except my cable! You – will – not – cut – it!'

'Sorry!' I shouted, and waved my hand. But he'd gone, breaking off the only conversation we ever had as cleanly as Sohan Singh had sliced through the wire. For it was only a wire – a length of flex acting as a personal contact, looping down into the water and up onto the hard, quite independent of his signals equipment. I gathered later that the Navy fouled the line at frequent intervals and kept a spare reel of flex in a shelter on the jetty, also that he, himself, never came ashore to take up that, or any other matter.

John Parsons, the leaner and swarthier of the Signals Twins, had been on the hard, listening to the ship-to-shore exchanges with some amusement, clad, as he often was, in an old bush-jacket, a soiled pair of battledress trousers cut just below the knee, and heavy brown boots; an attire which always made him seem more expansive.

'I can see his point,' I said sympathetically. 'Have you had any contact with him?'

'Well, actually, I'm one of the few who's had the chance to see his garden. Bjorn heard, God knows how, that I was keen on plants and had my own plot. He sent a strange message via one of his lascars to Selfridge, who was then Turner's Number One, asking if he'd get me to come up the wheelhouse. Anyway, I took it up . . . They swung me aboard, and I clambered across the gap. It was an extraordinary sight!

He's acquired a great variety of tropical plants at various ports of call, and being static, so to speak, he's got a flourishing greenhouse up there. I'm more interested in food plants, but I helped him identify several he was uncertain about. He's got a Honolulu Wood Rose, a sort of yellow Morning Glory. It's spread beyond the wheelhouse and over some of the scaffolding the Ceylon chaps put up.'

'Have you been back?'

'No. Not once! As you've just seen, he doesn't even acknowledge me.'

'What did you mean by your "plot"?'

'Which way are you going? . . . I'll show you. I'm going there anyway, as you can see,' he slapped his trousers. 'It's on the edge of the airstrip, this end; used to belong to the AW Company, but, like everyone else, they tried quite unsuitable plants.'

'I know, Box has been finding the snags!'

'Watch what the locals do,' he explained, as we walked across to see the results of his chief recreation, apart from bridge. 'Maize, yes, but use their varieties. Not much point my growing it, apart from corn-on-the-cob of an evening. It's their fruits and leaves I've been interested in, they've got most of the nutrients we need.'

As we crossed the coral runway, he pointed ahead to the roughly cleared strips which made up his palm-sheltered garden, a tangle of greenery.

'That,' he said, 'is what we should all be growing.' We walked over to the tangle of evergreen shrubs, on some of which, among large kidney-shaped, leathery leaves, were long clusters of grape-like fruit, some green, others turning an almost violet colour.

'Sea grapes, quite edible, and they resist salt-spray. You'll find 'em on tropical islands all over the world . . . and *those* are not just for show,' he said, seeing me eyeing the long, vivid red tails hanging from some of the darker shrubs. 'That's chenille, you can cook and eat the younger leaves.' His enthusiasm grew as we examined a surprising variety of foliage and roots.

'I'll stay on for a bit,' he said. 'I'll let you know when I'm supplementing the goat and tinned carrot, you can sample some. I tried chenille on Smivvy, but there's no one more conservative when it comes to diet than a true Cockney. He told Ashy explicitly what he could do with it!'

It was good to get John Parsons on his own. He was not always at his best in the evenings. As we'd seen with Rosy, he could be touchy and intolerant.

Having come this far, it seemed a good idea to check on the other construction job we had on hand. Most of Bir Singh's platoon were involved, a cheerful, bantering group, reflecting the Jemadar's personality. This particular assignment was really John Gossard's pet project. He'd got the NOIC to agree to his plan for a proper cinema, open on three sides, with a firm floor for seating and a low roof and fixed screen to help the acoustics.

There were several reasons for this. The *Rajah* had delivered a selection of films, for both British and Indian consumption, rationed out half-weekly, with repeats of the more popular. Unfortunately the screen, usually suspended between a tree and a rickety pole, had been rolled-up during a rain squall and left on the ground for several days. The insects had done their worst, and the gaps they'd made were disconcerting. We'd seen "In Which We Serve" on a number of occasions, but there was a limit to the enjoyment we could get from Noel Coward, cap rakishly tilted, making his dramatic declaration from the sloping deck through lips enlarged and distorted by a tree-trunk fifteen feet beyond the gap in the screen.

We'd also received a small crate of classical records, which John Gossard felt deserved reasonable amplification. Much of the sound had been lost to space from the old outdoor speakers. So, with the help of the Maldivians, expert at *kajjan* thatching, we were given the task of building the cinema . . . There was ghoulish pleasure in adding "Cinema Construction" to the weekly events recorded in the War Diary, returned at intervals to the Depot, and wondering whether Bentinck and Dawson still thought it had been worthwhile creaming off some of their best craftsmen to enrich our leisure hours. By now, I could hardly believe that only a few months ago I'd been depending on equipment drops in the jungle . . . it was a different world!

Organised leisure was important, however. Sikhs have a particular skill at hockey, stemming from stick-and-ball games in villages throughout the Punjab. The airstrip, seldom in use, provided a firm surface for inter-platoon contests, from which Jemadar Arjan Singh produced a side none of the other units could match. It was also an opportunity to get to know individuals, and confirm that though, as yet, we could hardly boast of engineering achievements, the unit had an accord which owed much to the experience of Bulwant Singh.

The same could hardly be said about the Mess. One situation in particular has begun to weigh on us all, the waywardness of Rosy Sinclair, and the inability of Philip Shuttleworth to cope with it.

Smivvy was the one chap in the Mess who *could* cope with Rosy. For one thing he could drink virtually any amount of anything with anyone, and who better than a genuine Cockney to counter Rosy's growing acidity with sharp repartee? At times the voice of the Raj and the ripostes of the East End docks were like a well-rehearsed double-act.

'Why you should address your men in that uncouth fashion I can't imagine! I heard you by the jetty this morning, two pips flashin' and a voice like a rusty saw shouting "Straighten it up you farts or I'll drop in on your bleedin' 'eads!" Surely you can learn to give orders properly!'

'Proper.'

'What?'

'Proper. You speak properly. I speak proper!'

'You're an arrogant little sod. You give the impression of wanting everyone to fit in with your own uncouth ideas. Pin-ups in the Mess, greeting the NOIC with your cap stuck on a bollard, insulting Number One . . . You seem to think you're running the island!'

'Yeah! Always 'noo I'd 'ave an a'oll of me own one day. First girl I 'ad was called Coral, and me Mum, Lil, was nicknamed "Lily of Laguna" by 'er boyfriend . . . got to look for the signs Rosy, got to read the tea-leaves!' . . . and so it went on.

But no one else could handle Rosy, least of all Philip Shuttleworth in the Battery. In reality Philip could safely have ignored him, and coped with the widespread deployment of his gun-crews even if he'd had only Ian and the VCOs. Ashwell was virtually 2 i/c in any case and responsible for the gun positions on Maladu and Havadu, in the far north, while the VCOs commanded a fixed gun-site on the tiny island of Funahera, and did spells there in rotation . . . which is what we must have seen on that first excursion with the Company boat.

Philip was determined to make Rosy take some responsibility, so put him in charge of the gun-sites at the southern end of Manu itself, positions only taken up in an emergency. They were tersely rude to each other – when they spoke. Shuttleworth's unimaginative bluntness gave Rosy nothing to respond to, whereas he would liven up with Smivvy as an adversary, and enjoyed it.

After the *British Sceptre* incident the NOIC had devised a system of joint-Service alerts. In particular, he cast an informed eye over deployment exercises by the Gunners, and one afternoon signalled the code for Shuttleworth to concentrate all his mobile artillery in the southern approaches. The guns rolled in from Maladu and southward from Havadu, past our bridge-strengthening party. Shuttleworth tore along the narrow coastal road towards Rosy's southernmost position, accompanied by the NOIC and his escort, stop-watches in hand, as it were. They were met by a slow-moving convoy, as Rosy retreated, taking his guns northward . . . All Philip had done was to pass him the codeword, and all Rosy had done was to misinterpret it. Mild though Turner appeared, the Gunners received a spectacular rocket.

Shuttleworth's response proved disastrous. He decided to order Rosy to do a spell on Funahera island; remote, though not, of course, out of touch, the detachment there had both RT and a small boat at their disposal.

We'd never visited the island, but rumour had it that the gun guarding the northern approaches had been struck early in the Boer War, had limited ammunition, and that no one had dared fire a practice round. Apocryphal no doubt, but it was that sort of place.

A week after the cock-up and ensuing confusion, Rosy, who'd hardly left the Mess, set off in the Battery's boat to relieve the VCO on Funahera. He had with him four Indian Gunners, a bedding roll, a trunk, and a case of assorted bottles.

Shuttleworth, mouth open, apprehensively watched his departure from the verandah outside the NOIC's Office. Apprehensive because Rosy had organised his own movement without a word of recrimination. He'd simply laid on his equipment and his precious supplies, and then departed.

Philip felt uneasy about it all. He cautiously re-read his Order which had specifically detailed Captain Sinclair to accompany the detachment on its weekly stint on the island, in case he'd failed to make it clear that it was a week-long exile.

On Monday nothing happened . . . On Tuesday a personal chitti addressed to **'Major P. J. Shuttleworth, RA'** arrived by boat from Funahera:

'Unless you personally order me to return to Manu island forthwith, I shall have no option other than to report your shortcomings, your inability to effect adequate communication, the cover-up of your error on 20 Apr 45, and your subsequent unforgivable behaviour to your immediate superiors.'

Philip carried it about with him, showed it, with a forced jocularity, to all and sundry in the Mess, but could be seen surreptitiously looking at it

100

from time to time during the evening . . . Early Wednesday morning a formal letter was delivered to Naval HQ, addressed to **'NOIC HMS** *Taltara'*:

> *'Sir*
> *Unless you take steps to ensure my immediate return to Manu island, I shall assume that the distressful episode on 20 Apr 45 was due to collusion between your good self and OC 89 Battery RIA, for some reason known only to yourselves, and shall be obliged to take appropriate action.*
> *I am, Sir, your obedient servant etc . . .'*

On Thursday afternoon another formal communication was delivered to Naval HQ addressed to **'The Flag Officer Commanding, Ceylon – through NOIC HMS** *Taltara'* . . . immaculately written on a neatly folded strip of bumf.

> *'Sir,*
> *In due deference to your somewhat exalted position, I am writing this on the shiny side . . .'* it began.

On Friday morning a Naval patrol vessel was sent to take him off. The NOIC, the MO, and Shuttleworth were in close conference for most of the morning, and by Saturday it was known that Rosy's orderly had taken his belongings to Naval HQ.

Rosy himself remained there until Tuesday midday when, as the NOIC must have anticipated, a small cargo ship anchored off the jetty. Eight hours later he was on his way to Colombo.

Before we left the atoll Ian Ashwell had a cheerful letter from him, sent from the pleasant hill-station of Ootacamund, though it didn't say what he was doing there. Philip Shuttleworth did *not* hear from him, and had long since been informed that there would be no replacement.

CHAPTER TWELVE

Ants, Goats, Hens and Turtles

If you have no trouble buy a goat.
French Proverb

No goat ever died of hunger.
Persian Proverb

A green and white island, a sparkling lagoon, an absorbing pastime . . . and a fading concern about our true role. Things seemed to have settled down well. Yet as week followed week with trivial tasks and relative inactivity, small signs of restlessness began to appear. The *arzi* parades were unearthing more and more minor irritations.

In most units there seemed to be one or two *arzi* addicts. With us it was Sapper Ishar Singh. He was young, with only a fuzz of beard, but full of his family's rights and wrongs. The Subedar knew the background of this particular village feud by heart, for Ishar Singh came from a *tehsil* not far from Rampur, and I imagine the Sikhs discussed it among themselves.

Each Friday we re-enacted the same routine, starting with Prem Singh's forefinger jabbing the *arzi* book.

'Sapper Ishar Singh is next, Sahib . . . *Ishar Singh idhar ao!*'

'Well, Ishar Singh, you have a problem I believe.'

He furrowed his brow and looked extremely worried; and then, as if I'd never heard it before, began to spell it out in precise detail.

'I have no problem, Sahib. It is my brother who has the problem.'

'Tell me exactly what it is Ishar Singh.' . . . as if I didn't know!

'My brother's name is Mohan Singh. He has one field next to the field of Ram Singh. There is a canal between.' He held his hands in parallel to show me the space separating the properties.

At this point Prem Singh would explain to me that this was not a big canal, or even a brick-lined canal like the one that flowed across the village land, but a much smaller *nala*, an unlined channel which carried water only when the summer crops needed irrigating. Then he would turn to the plaintiff:

'Go on Ishar Singh, the Sahib understands.'

'Before the *kharif* crop is to be irrigated Ram Singh is building up his ridges to plant his grain and is cleaning out the canal. This is his job, it is not my brother's job.'

Prem Singh would interrupt . . . 'Not canal. It is *nala*.'

'Hasn't Ram Singh been clearing the *nala*?' I would ask.

'Yes, Sahib, he is clearing the *nala*, but each time Ram Singh is cutting from my brother's land and is putting the earth onto his own side. The canal . . .'

'*Nala . . . nala!*' from Prem Singh.

'The *nala* is moving each time, little by little, across my brother's land.'

Prem Singh would then explain to me that this was often a source of dispute.

'I understand,' I said. 'How far has it been moved this year, Ishar Singh?'

He would spread his palms to indicate a few feet. 'This far, Sahib. Each time it is this far.'

'Very well, we will send a letter and ask for this to be investigated. Right?'

'That is good, Sahib, but the *patwari* must charge my brother less tax on his land, and must charge Ram Singh more tax.'

'I will make a report, Ishar Singh. But it will be some time before we can expect an answer.'

'*Achha bat Sahib*,' he would say, shaking his head back and forth, and off he would go, outwardly contented for another week.

I'd tried to point out to him that we'd made several reports about it all. But he always countered with, 'Sahib will please be sending another. It is only if we keep telling Ram Singh that he will stop doing this.'

He was well-meaning; it kept him happy; and Prem Singh and the Subedar knew this as well as I did.

However, from time to time the real rogues would appear, the ones that tried it on . . . like Sapper Sunda Singh.

In his case it all began at the Clothing Condemnation Parade, held by the Quartermaster. We had a limited quantity of replacement clothing, so the thinning blouses with frayed collars had to serve a great deal longer than at Depot.

By inclination Sunda Singh was not just smart, he was dapper. Sweat patches soon discoloured the khaki shirts and jungle-green blouses, so he took his stained battledress blouse to be replaced. But Pritap Singh would have none of it.

A week later the battledress top appeared again. Sunda Singh held it out carefully at arm's length, as though displaying a choice roll of cloth, and turned it about to show that the back had almost completely gone.

A long-serving VCO like Pritap Singh would recognise a deliberate tear at a glance, but this wasn't torn, it had simply disintegrated. He turned to the self-assured Sunda Singh.

'This cannot have rotted like this in one week. Even rough treatment at the *dhobi ghat* wouldn't cause it to fall apart like this.'

'No, Sahib, this is the work of ants. I washed my blouse at the *dhobi ghat* and laid it out to dry on a fallen palm trunk. There is an ant's nest in the trunk, and the ants have eaten my shirt.' He stood confidently, feet apart, looking the towering Pritap Singh straight in the eye.

The Jemadar put him on a charge.

So up came Sunda Singh, spick and span in his new battledress top, properly at ease before my scorpion-ridden desk, beard immaculately rolled, moustache twisted, and a half smile on his face. The Jemadar did the questioning.

'The *dhobi ghat* is specially built for you to wash your clothes . . . where is it?'

The answer was pat and precise, with a lift of the chin, 'It is behind 3 Platoon huts, Sahib.'

'Where did you place your shirt for the sun to dry it?'

'On a tree trunk, Sahib, but there were ants there, Sahib.'

'You are quite right, Sunda Singh, I've seen the hole in the trunk, it's full of ants. How far is the tree trunk from the *dhobi ghat*?'

'Twenty yards, Sahib.'

'How far?'

'Thirty yards, Sahib.'

'How far? You've done your basic training, Sunda Singh, you know how to estimate distance. How far?'

'Fifty yards, Sahib.'

'That is a long way to go to find a place to dry your shirt! You must have looked for a long time to find a hole full of ants, Sunda Singh!'

'Yes, Sahib, a long time.' He switched his steady gaze from the Jemadar to me, as if awaiting verdict and sentence.

So Sunda Singh did his extra duties and drills . . . but at least he looked extremely smart.

The element of boredom was not unique to the other ranks. There was an edginess in the Mess. It had taken a while to settle down after Rosy's departure. Then, unfortunately, our more cordial relationship with John Parsons met with a severe setback. Box caught the full force of it, which was just as well for he could generally smooth things down, though in this case not very effectively. It was doubly unfortunate, for in fact we sympathised with John and blamed it all on whatever malign influence determined that whenever things were on an even keel Bachan Singh would find some way to rock the boat!

It had happened one afternoon as Box walked from the jetty to check on the finishing touches to the cinema-cum-social centre. As he'd emerged from the greenery onto the coral airstrip, a flurry of goats erupted from the undergrowth on the far side, leaping and bounding through the palms, before settling down to more placid activities, some nibbling at the fronds on the surface, some wandering on, others turning back to where a distraught-looking soldier had appeared from among the bushes.

Immediately recognising Bachan Singh, Box went over to find what was wrong and see if he could help. Before he'd gone more than a few paces, a taller figure appeared, gazing about and, surprised at seeing Box, bellowed, 'Are you with this lunatic? Come and see what his bloody goats have done! You should bloody well keep them wherever they're supposed to be!'

As Box explained, Bachan Singh and his charges would have had no idea that Parsons' garden, with its succulent shrubs, was anything more than indigenous vegetation . . . but John had arrived to find them happily munching his root crops and standing on two legs to nibble away at the Sea Grapes. In reality they hadn't done all that much damage, but he'd laid into Bachan Singh and his animals, and, illogically, Box and I were deemed equally culpable.

Neither of us mentioned it to the Subedar, but you could keep little from him, especially on an island this size. So two days later he let us know that he'd given the Company Goatherd more specific instructions.

The Information Room had come into its own now that the War in Europe seemed to be coming to an end. Messages received by Naval HQ and snippets gleaned from the old Mess radio were typed out and pinned-up among Smivvy's Lana Turner profiles.

The Company also had an "Information Room", partitioned-off in the Stores; though, like our mandatory Current Affairs talks, the contents made little impact on the average Sapper. Despite their travels, most of them retained their parochial, almost isolationist, attitude concerning the Punjab and its relations with the wider world.

While victory in the West seemed imminent, there appeared to be no end to the war against Japan, and the possibility of mounting an attack on Japanese-controlled Malaya was a frequent topic of conversation, with speculation about the role of the atoll.

There was a great deal of activity in the Indian Ocean, and the atoll sheltered or serviced a variety of vessels in quick succession . . . two oil tankers, several small cargo ships, and a cruiser which stayed long enough to put ashore a soccer side which beat a scratch island eleven, and a hockey team which was massacred by 725's Sikhs.

Ozzie was obviously more affected by the increased naval activity than the rest of us, and had been having a hectic time as Beachmaster – by Kulu standards. He switched off in the evenings by taking Rosy's place in prolonged sessions with Smivvy, but without Rosy's cutting edge. However, one crack at the Poms was taken at more than face value by Ian Ashwell, who was looking for an excuse to pass on his job as Mess Secretary.

After dinner one evening Ian was writing at one of the card tables at the far end of the Mess, plagued by ear-flies. Whatever you did, these minute black flies would return to zoom into the ear cavities with a high-pitched vibrating hum. You had only to be a bit tense or off-colour for them to set the nerves tingling. Ozzie, sitting by the bar, interrupted him.

'Git a more imaginative menu, Ashy. Typical bloody Pom, all you do's open a few more cans. Up near Wiluna, where me old man worked, if we got brassed off with mutton stew we'd shoot a few roos, or strangle a few bloody wallabies. Use your initiative, Ashy, catch a flamin' turtle or blow a few edible fish out of the sea, not that bony crap we've had for the last few weeks!'

Instead of lifting two fingers in response, as all good Poms should do when assailed by Aussie invective, Ashwell scooped up his papers and walked towards the door.

'Come on Ashy!' pleaded Ozzie. 'Don't be so bloody wet. I don't mind it, really. It's just the other poor Poms I'm worried about. They haven't been weaned on the sort of grub we git in the outback. I hate to see them suffer!'

The following morning Ashwell, suffering from prickly heat as well as flies, informed the breakfasters that they could find another Mess Secretary, and walked out with the sort of gesture he should have used in the first place.

As with the Grand Prix nonsense, it was generally felt that Gilbert might be the man for the job, or the least likely to refuse it, and before the evening was out he'd agreed to take it on.

Taking Ozzie's disparagements seriously, he canvassed for suggestions to cheer up the menu. One proposal, uninspired but sensible, was to acquire more chicken. Most units had a well-stocked run, so Gilbert was empowered to buy-in a few hens, and the following day made his first purchases from Daya Singh's flourishing flock.

He and his driver arrived at the Company Office soon after lunch and announced his intention. So we collected Daya Singh and went over to his now imposing wired-in run. Gilbert stood back as he unfastened the door and they ducked inside. He peered warily at the agitated hens and pointed randomly at one or two as they fluttered about the cage. Daya Singh said something I couldn't catch but, seeing me watching, Gilbert pressed his face to the wire.

'Your chappie says I need some twine. We have to tie their legs together. Anything I can use?'

Daya Singh pointed to a length of frayed string looped over a nail by the door, so I jerked it free and pushed it through the mesh. He picked up two hens, put them under his arms and handed them to Gilbert, one at a time. Held by Daya Singh, they were motionless bundles of feathers, staring about them. Handled by Gilbert, they immediately sprang into life, twisting, flapping, and squawking.

Eventually Gilbert managed to pinion six of them and bring them out in pairs, heads downward, and handed them to his Dogra driver, who threw them, somewhat disdainfully, into the back of his bull-nosed 15-cwt. He'd been watching Gilbert's efforts through the wire, and I had the feeling that, as a Dogra in Sikh territory, he thought Gilbert had let the side down.

'Thanks,' said Gilbert, breezily. 'See you later on.' And off they set along the track towards the airstrip.

Daya Singh scattered some food for the rest of the flock and fastened the door of the run. I was just turning back to the Office when there was the sound of fierce braking . . . At the end of the track I could see Gilbert and his driver leap out and plunge into the undergrowth. A moment later Gilbert backed out again, looking up at the palms. He then turned towards the truck and lunged at the tailboard. I could just see the second pair of hens taking off to the right.

'Are their wings clipped?' I asked Daya Singh, pointing to the hen-house. He looked at me in astonishment, but said nothing. I struggled for alternatives. 'Are their wings chopped?'

'Sahib?'

'Are their wings cut?' He half smiled, but said nothing.

'Can the birds fly?' His face lit up.

'Yes, Sahib, they can fly, but wire covers the whole *murghi-khana*, so they are not flying away.' He, too, thought I was pretty unintelligent.

Gilbert arrived at the Mess clutching the unfortunate survivors. From time to time we would see the others pecking about in the bush, or peering down at us from the branches in a superior manner.

Nevertheless Gilbert had his successes, even if the results of his imagination were blunted by the limitations of his helpmates.

Martin Welland, who helped to distribute weekly rations to the Maldivians, had become friendly with a number of fishermen and their families. One evening he informed Gilbert that a particular friend of his, Abdul Didi, might be able to bring in a turtle, if Gilbert would like one. Gilbert leapt at the idea.

So, about a week after the liberation of the chicken, an outrigger arrived from Makofulu, its single sail billowing in the steady easterlies as it towed in two very large turtles. The gourmets licked their lips, and the card players began playing for the shells.

A large turtle carries a remarkable quantity of flesh for a smallish Mess, but the cooks hardly made the best culinary use of it. Turtle soup was on everyone's mind, but it was terrible. They tried stewing the carapace and using the stock, but fell down badly on the "richly flavoured with herbs". Genuine gourmets, according to Gilbert, thought highly of its flippers. So we had one braised with diluted port, courtesy of Wings, who was invited over as a connoisseur, and another with sticky green – "spirits of mint" Gilbert called it. Either way they were disgusting.

Eventually it was decided to soak the remainder in fresh water, detach as much as possible and boil that. Some was left to dry in the sun, but even so, it didn't offer a great deal. We had it straight boiled, re-fried, sautéd in ghi, and what Gilbert, ever imaginative, called "à la Nicoise", which seemed to be plastered with once-hot congealed tomato sauce. Finally we had it curried.

'God sends meat, but the Devil sends cooks,' said Box, trying to nettle Gilbert into bandying quotations . . . but for once Gilbert was silent. The turtle went on and on, but at least we got rid of it before the VE Day festivities.

CHAPTER THIRTEEN

Waving Antennae

Where there are no women there are no good manners.
J. W. Goethe: *Elective Affinities II* (1805)

Hostilities in Europe ceased at midnight on the 8th of May, and on Kulu Atoll Victory was celebrated by formal parades, hockey matches, and wrestling displays organised by Naik Mukand Singh – to the casual observer a most inappropriate way of celebrating peace – and by a great deal of boisterousness.

The Sunderland being elsewhere, a "Grand Fly Past" was performed by Wings in his old Walrus. Several risked trips with him during the day . . . a frightening venture, for with the extra weight it was touch and go when it came to clearing the palms at the end of the runway, especially towards evening when Wings was screaming 'Tally Ho!' as he took off. Nevertheless, trundling low over the islands was a memorable experience. Once the weird assortment of occupants was diminished by distance, the atoll was overwhelmingly beautiful. From the air the deep blue lagoon seemed almost purple, the wide outer shelf a brilliant interlacing of delicate greens, blues and white, with patches of crimson corals, while white foam formed an irregular necklace about each of the islands . . . It was day to remember.

Further celebrations took place on May the 13th, on the occasion of Churchill's Victory Broadcast. At eight in the evening, our time, his speech was relayed to the troops in the newly completed cinema, where Churchill's oratory lost a lot in a precised translation by the Dogra Jemadar! The officers mostly gathered about sets in the Wardroom and the Mess.

We'd considered various preludes to the speech and the following

110

celebrations. The most ambitious, Ozzie's idea for a warm-up hopping race, was abandoned after Benjy Bryant had all but lost an ear. "Hopping" was a euphemism. We'd come across a number of spare Met balloons. The idea was to attach them to the shoulders and inflate them sufficiently to allow competitors to leap down the runway in enormous bounds. Ozzie, being no fool, persuaded Benjy to try one out; but it was not easy to control the inflation. When we let go of him, he went soaring off like a whizz-bang, hit a nearby palm tree about five feet up and had to be stitched by Doc Walsh.

The Broadcast itself was impressive, the celebrations momentous. The speech went on rather longer than we'd bargained for, however, and triggered another Aussie-Pom confrontation. Towards the end, the old man pontificated:

'Though holiday rejoicing is necessary to the human spirit, yet it must add to the strength and resilience with which every man and woman turns again to the work they have to do.'

At which Ozzie leapt to his feet, looking intently about him, over sunglasses pulled forward on his nose: 'Sho it shall,' he declared in Churchillian tones, 'Sho it shall! I shall go forward with resholution. I shall triumph in the bush and by the beaches. Tonight I shall ride forth in triumph in the Grand Prix. Too bloody right! Tonight I shall pish on Forresht-hyphen-Hill. I have shabotaged his shouped-up monstroshity, so tonight we enter this field of human conflict in my old banger!'

He tipped back his drink and threw the glass against the bar with a crash . . . Eventually they roared around in turn in Ozzie's truck, and Forrest-Hill beat him comfortably . . . Half an hour later Ozzie was asleep on one of the old MT seats, his back to the insect-ridden panels at the side of the Mess.

He was, in fact, the second casualty of the evening, discounting the injured Benjy, who now resembled Claud Rains as the original "Invisible Man", bloodshot eyes peering out from beneath layers of bandage. Box had brought Furry along to join in the festivities. Early on, someone had hoisted him onto the bar and poured him an ashtray-full of sticky green. He went at it like a dog possessed, lapping and looking foolishly around, and lapping again, until Box lifted him off for safety. He squeaked once or twice, tottered towards the foot of the bar, and went out like a light, as if an unseen hand had inverted him.

A week later the whole tenor of life on the atoll was disturbed by a signal from SS *Ryde*, a small general cargo vessel which would be putting-in for a couple of days. She was carrying two QA Nursing Officers who'd recently been decorated. They would come ashore as guests of the Royal Navy. This may sound simply a pleasant formality, but most of the island's Service population had been without female company for a very long time. So that when Lieutenants Joan Renshaw and Maggie Rutherford stepped ashore late one afternoon antennae began waving throughout the western islands.

The Captain had invited a number of us to the Wardroom to meet them. Considering the customary casual attendance at the island's social functions, it was remarkable how, prompt at seven, the Wardroom began filling up. The floral decoration was somewhat sparse. One might have thought that Equatorial atolls were rich in exotic blossoms. Dorothy Lamour was seldom without her frangipani . . . but all that survived in the Wardroom annexe were straggly bougainvilleas and a solitary bright red hibiscus. John Parson's kitchen garden was probably more attractive, if closely examined.

It was some twenty minutes before I had the chance to talk with either of our guests. Maggie, gingery, freckled and capable-looking, was in her late-twenties, with an uncomplicated "jolly hockey sticks" manner. Wings had discovered that her father was a regular Indian Army officer and the family home Rawalpindi. She'd been at school in England, but had returned to share the outdoor pursuits of her father and two brothers, which had included the rigours of *shikar* trips into the Himalayan foothills. This put her answers to my tentative questions in perspective.

'What brings you here?' seemed a reasonable opener.

'Should say "a small cargo ship" I suppose; but you mean where've we come from?'

'Well, yes.'

'Answer's Diego Garcia. We've been coming back from East Africa in stages. Unfortunately it was "all change" at DG – for the second time.'

'Why the second time?'

'Got marooned there last year.' Her pleasant matter-of-fact manner reduced small-talk to the minimum, but tended to leave gaps.

'How do you mean marooned?'

'Well the ship that picked us up dropped us on DG. We were stranded there for several weeks.'

'Picked you up from where?'

'From the sea – torpedoed. We were jolly lucky,' she added. 'Lucky to be picked up. I think most of us were rescued. We were coming from Mombasa and they had a go at us. From DG it was back to East Africa . . . Now we're on course again.'

She seemed to have written-off the lengthy disruption of her trip to India as "one of those things".

'So now you're going to join the family in 'Pindi?'

'No. I'm going to Ceylon. There's no one at home now. Daddy's gone to Chungking, of all places! Mummy's always off somewhere – social job in Delhi this time. From what I can gather, she's been helping to turn the Red Fort into a transit camp, but she does tend to be vague, seems a jolly odd place to choose. And the boys have been away all through the War.'

It sounded as though the family in Rawalpindi were all out for the day, and mother, being vague, might just have forgotten to say when they'd be back.

I wanted to find out more about her father's visit to Chiang Kai-Shek, but our guests were in demand. Charles Holland, a Flight Lieutenant with the Sunderland crew on Havadu, broke into the conversation. This was something in itself, for Holland hardly ever visited the Mess or the Wardroom. The RAF contingent were away a lot, of course, and most atollians assumed that the Seychelles, Mombasa and Colombo offered rather more than Kulu! Nevertheless the RAF was now showing interest and Holland was soon recalling his visits to East Africa.

I moved towards Joan Renshaw. She too had been adrift for several days. In contrast to the forthright Maggie, she was small, slim, and fair-haired, looking equally capable, but bubbly . . . and completely surrounded. Their combined effect on our isolated community was unmistakable. As might be expected, Doc Walsh appeared to have spent even more time trimming his beard; Holland had appeared from Havadu; and then there was Smivvy who, working closely with the Navy, had presumably asked himself. He was wearing a clean bush-jacket and had pressed his trousers, though the creases were out of line and doubled, as if, in the time-honoured way, he'd slept on them, but had had a restless night. His mousey hair, which he usually cut himself, was sleeked back with something or other – spiky but gleaming.

He'd tackled Lieutenant Renshaw with some confidence, and seemed genuinely concerned that his attractive offer had been turned down.

'Couldn't say I'd show 'er me etchin's, I don't 'ave any. Said I'd show 'er me shells.'

'You don't have any shells, Smivvy.'

'You'd've lent me yours, Martin; you've got a smashing collection!' But even this imaginary description of my display hadn't tempted her.

During the evening the NOIC, recalling appropriate formalities from earlier days, decided that their departure would be attended by a small, but well turned-out section of military – a small detail from the Dogras. So the following afternoon saw a number of the *Ryde's* officers, looking rather embarrassed, and two glisteningly smart QAs, progressing somewhat stiffly towards the jetty with its file of Dogras and immaculate ratings.

Timed to perfection, the only individual capable of reducing Service formality to basic human values shuffled steadily across their path, head bowed, a laden haversack across his shoulders, from each side of which protruded two small hooves.

'Oh! Isn't he sweet!' Joan Renshaw, breaking ranks, skipped over to pat the bulging contents, much to the bewilderment of Bachan Singh, whose burden, recently dropped amid the greenery, was just another recruit for his diminishing herd.

The NOIC beamed; the guests, chatting freely, sauntered casually down the jetty; and the Dogras continued to stand rigidly to attention.

CHAPTER FOURTEEN

Round the Bend

There is no happiness without action.
Benjamin Disraeli: *Lothair III* (1870)

He maketh the deep boil like a pot.
Job XLI 31 (c.325 BC)

The Catalina continued to arrive once a week, bringing mail and an occasional bonus. In mid-June it splashed into the lagoon with a fine selection of books to add to the tatty Mess library. Gilbert had the advantage of being able to read and re-read his specialist subject with growing interest and awareness, and we'd borrowed from him. But there was a limit to ingesting undiluted Gothic, or original Anglo-Saxon, though evidence of its influence on Smivvy's vocabulary was enlightening! But the real surprise was the arrival of Jock Covington with a couple of REME officers for an overnight stay. We'd trained together in England, and he'd come out a month or so after us. After a spell in the Arakan we'd lost touch, but he was now commanding a team inspecting equipment in various parts of south-east Asia.

He'd come over in the early evening, and we sat by the beach with a drink, watching the sun dip rapidly onto the horizon . . . a great red disc, expanding, then sinking as if it had been torpedoed.

'God, you're lucky!' he said to Box. 'What a way to spend the War!' Though he'd quickly assessed the problems of an active Company "stranded" in what he called "Ocean Bases". We filled him in with some of the more bizarre happenings that seemed to typify service on Kulu.

'Yes,' he'd said, after hearing details of Rosy's abrupt departure. 'I've realised that you're round the bend,' then somewhat abruptly swivelled towards Box and wagged a finger. 'You'll have to take them off, you know. I've told the NOIC they're quite ridiculous, and he agrees.'

'What . . .?' said Box, speechless for once; obviously floored by the change of attitude.

'You serious, Jock?' I said . . . but by then he was laughing like a drain, and reaching for his glass.

A week or so back someone suggested revealing how near the brink we were by making suitable insignia – a neat flash to be worn by our Kulu-based military. After much deliberation we'd gone for a black diamond embroidered with a single bend – a shallow white "C". The idea caught on in the Mess, and Sewa Singh, our aptly named tailor, had turned out a pair per officer on his splendid machine, helped by his friend, Mohan Singh, using an old Singer borrowed from the AW Company. On each sleeve, beneath the regimental flash, there was now a clear message – 'round the bend!'

'Pulling your leg!' he said. 'Keep 'em on. Most of us have qualified for them over the last few years: it summarises what this nonsense is all about! In fact, if you've got a spare pair I'll take a couple with me. It'll be interesting to see what Mountbatten, or anyone else at Trinco, thinks I'm wearing. You need something to grab their attention!'

Before he left we probed about the future. He'd told John Gossard, in his official capacity, that in view of the rapid build-up to remove the Japs from Malaya we should keep up battle training and concentrate on demolitions. The NOIC, obviously aware that most of our tasks had been cosmetic rather than constructive engineering, had agreed that we put one platoon each week entirely on battle training. So, from then on, every few days the flags were out and bullets whistled from dugouts in the storm beaches through targets on the reef and into the breakers.

Ozzie's duties as Beachmaster, arduous as they were for short periods, left him with intervals when he had little to do and he liked to go out with the shooting squads. He regaled all and sundry with particulars of his marksmanship in the wild outback of the north-west. After a dramatic account of stopping a charging buffalo, which had reverted to the wild, Box handed him a rifle and a clip.

'Have a go, Ozzie. The target's pretty static, so it may not suit you, of course.'

But it wasn't just bull. Ozzie could shoot! He was deadly accurate. As he stood watching the white jets of spray thrown up on the outer reef, out came the Aussie banter:

'Where's yer ping-pong balls? Make a proper fairground job of it, Boxy. Give us a worthwhile target!'

Demolitions were even more popular with the Sikhs. We went about looking for things to blow up. The most satisfactory was that symbol of our frustration, the half-completed oil tank, fortunately at a safe distance from the others.

Jemadar Bir Singh was an explosives fanatic, so we turned him loose on an old jetty on the seaward side of Maladu. The idea was to blast realisitic gaps and use what was left standing for further training. Everything went without a hitch. Three simultaneous explosions cracked out and reverberated across the island. But the reward was more than the satisfaction at a job well done: soon the Sappers were scooping up rock cod, coral trout, and a host of gaudy fish stunned by the shock-waves. Best of all were the octopuses. There must have been a colony of them, if that's how they live . . . I laid claim to them on behalf of Gilbert and the cooks.

This time we were onto a good thing. Martin Welland suggested the Greek cook attached to the Wardroom would know what to do with them . . . none of the hit-and-miss we'd had with the turtles.

We went in search of the alleged expert and discovered Leading Seaman Dandoulakis in his singlet, opening a tin – an unpromising start! But his eyes lit up at the mention of octopus. Not only did he advise, but in exchange for two small ones – 'is good small'- he came over and prepared them for us. Delicately flavoured sliced rings of tentacles, he'd even brought a little garlic and olive oil, these were just the start. He also helped our unimaginative cooks select from the fish which had found its way to the Mess.

We toasted Jock Covington, without whose advice the octopuses would have remained submerged, busily increasing their colony, if that's what they did.

Unfortunately we ran short of explosives and, as the Captain was unwilling to let us tap Naval reserves, restricted fishing to the odd slab of guncotton, and even turned to using a baited cage and trap-door; but the bag was small by comparison.

On the serious side, the switch to more combative occupations had positive influences on general morale. The effects of battle training on the Company were astonishing. I think we'd all become lethargic without realising it. Bachan Singh and his goats, steadily dwindling in number, were apt to be disturbed by green-clad figures crawling about the waste-ground in battledress, webbing, and camouflaged helmets; and as soon as a platoon had a spell of battle-training, the numbers at *arzi* parade and the number of complaints dropped. Things were reverting to normal . . . Jock Covington's visit had paid off in more ways than one.

The last week in July, however, brought an unusual diversion. Over south-east Asia it was the wet monsoon season and during the past month there had been high humidity. Even when tempered by breeze, there was a closer, heavier feel. Clouds billowed-up by day and occasional squally showers swept the islands, lashing the lagoon, bending the palms and bringing the older coconuts cascading down. These seldom lasted long, and normally the Indian monsoon hardly affected the atoll; being Equatorial it escaped most of the severe cyclonic storms, though not necessarily their effects.

We'd arrived too late for the previous end-of-monsoon disturbances, but Benjy Bryant graphically described how in early October the swell from a distant cyclone submerged the island to a depth of several feet, so that his charpoy floated about in his hut! Ozzie, too, had missed these excesses and felt that Benjy was coming the old soldier, especially as he'd reckoned the island had dried out again in a few hours.

'Benjy,' he said, 'you're the glibbest line-shooter I've met since I left Fremantle. If you want to know about real storms Benjy my boy, ask me. I've been up north when the Willi-Willies set in . . .'

'Western Australia's not floating up to the gunwales in the ocean, Ozzie! I've seen this place bloody well submerged.'

And so it went on. But, yes, we were sceptical.

During mid-July the weather was still hot and close but not unduly capricious, though the sea had begun to roll-in in heavy swells. The deep opaque in-swillings over the coral shelf left little shelly terraces on the storm beaches as the tide fell. The Naval Met people attributed this to an intense cyclone far away to the north-east, and thought these conditions might persist for some time. However, we weren't affected in any particular way, and the Maldivian outriggers were about the lagoon as usual.

On the last Wednesday in July we were sitting outside our quarters in a couple of deck-chairs made by Sanichar Singh's disciples, using a length of old green canvas "borrowed" from the AW Company, proud possessions, symbolising our decadent sedentary life. Ajit Singh had just collected Furry for a walk, so we'd poured a beer and slumped back contentedly during the few minutes that passed for dusk. The red was fading from the western sky, the air unusually still. Flying-foxes were beginning to move about the palms, and voices were carrying clearly from the Company lines. We could hear Havidar Sohan Singh's high-pitched nattering and the shouts of laughter following his monologue.

'Sh!' said Box, quietly. Which surprised me, for I hadn't made a sound. 'Listen to the surf. I've never heard it quite like that.'

The sound of the breakers had long since become an accustomed, unheeded noise. But now, as we listened, there was a different pitch altogether, and dull thumps I couldn't remember hearing before. It was still low-tide, yet the water remained high enough to cover the coral on the shelf and break in gentle waves at the foot of the sloping storm-beach, ten feet away.

It was rapidly getting dark and we couldn't see any change in the line of white surf along the edge of the reef, but I agreed, there was a different quality of sound, and an eerie feel about the atmosphere, which was seldom as still as this.

At one-in-the-morning we must have woken simultaneously. Water was swilling over the storm-beach and pouring towards the centre of the island. In the room it was already inches deep, with a sound of lapping against the bathroom door.

I heard Box shout 'Furry', and squelch out to pull in the kennel. He came in by the back door carrying a wet dog which was trying to lick his face. At that moment Karam Singh appeared at the front, and we began putting things as high up as we could. I struggled into battledress and made for the lines, with a strong inflow of water swilling past. It was now a foot or so deep. The first thing I saw was a line of Sappers handling very passive birds from Daya Singh's chicken-run, making a better job of it than Gilbert had. There were lights everywhere. The Subedar and Pritap Singh came splashing out of the Stores, where a Section was already putting things on shelves and lifting sacks of vulnerable foodstuffs to safety.

'You've moved quickly, Subedar Sahib,' I said appreciatively.

'Yes, Sahib, we're putting any office equipment that should be moved onto HQ Platoon's charpoys.

'I see you've rescued the chickens; what about the goats?'

'Bachan Singh has gone in a truck to the compound to see if we have to move them. He has a squad to help him if need be.'

'Where are spare men assembling?'

'Those not needed are going to 3 Platoon huts, but the drivers are with the spare trucks by the *dhobi ghat*, to help move what may be necessary.'

As he spoke the water was audibly rushing over the barrier-beach, surging among the palms, and cascading through the Company lines almost at knee height. As we made for the office Prem Singh came wading towards us.

'HQ is saying this is a major storm surge and should last for two hours. The Company will please be in touch every half-hour, or report any emergency at once. They also say that 725 boat has been secured.'

Meanwhile, most of the Sappers were treating it as a huge joke. I could hear Jemadar Mangal Singh forcefully telling them to shut up, presumably because his 3 Platoon quarters were being invaded by odd bodies from other platoons.

Salt water continued to stream over the barrier in small swashes, but the depth over the island was not noticeably increasing, the water seemed to be holding at knee height. There was a lot of debris swilling about, notably coconuts and old husks, floating fronds, and bits of board; but any suggestion of alarm was visibly and audibly disappearing, and the noise from 3 Platoon huts increasing to the extent that the Subedar said, 'Excuse me, Sahib,' and strode off in the direction of the hilarity as purposefully as the waters would allow.

'I'm not surprised,' said Box. 'Reactions to a real threat are interesting, a nervous cheerfulness seems to set in. As I sloshed through the lines just now there was shriek like an animal in pain and a ghastly wheezing bray. I wondered what the hell it was; but even before I put my head through the door I could hear our beloved Teacher . . . Force Nine! He and Bir Singh were sitting, knees up on a packing case, tears running down their cheeks, speechless with laughter. So I waved in a "You all right?" sort of way and retreated.'

The Met chaps were now confident that the worst was over. I waded back to our quarters to see what the damage was, and found Karam Singh and Furry on the camp bed and Ajit Singh sitting on the chair with his feet up. It was too late to stop them trying to stand to attention, but I had time to confirm that the bed was not floating, nor had it floated . . . either Benjy had exaggerated, or his was a really exceptional storm surge!

By three in the morning no more water was coming over the beach barrier, and an hour or so later there were only wide individual pools on the road and about the huts. By early-morning Parade almost all the water had soaked into the coral and the vegetation was beginning to steam.

The debris included a great variety of marine life, most of it stranded. Small fishes, molluscs, and sea-snakes lay among the bushes. Crabs scuttled through the shrubby undergrowth. The lee slopes of the storm-beaches were deeply channelled and tapering mounds of coral fragments had been washed inland, while the roots of the glossy-leaved shrubs and low trees were even more exposed, though secure enough in the coarse material. Lines of hermit crabs, complete with their shell houses, were sitting on the lower branches as usual, though whether they'd clung on or had climbed back it was impossible to decide.

During the morning I asked the Subedar about the goats.

'Sapper Bachan Singh was very firm with the helpers,' he said, with some pride. 'He sent some of the small goats to HQ platoon, but after Parade returned them to the compound. Of course,' he added, 'he has fewer to look after, now so many have been eaten. Prem Singh has asked his friend at HQ when we might be getting a new delivery. He didn't know, but some say a supply ship is arriving in a few weeks.'

That was the first I'd heard of it, but rumours usually had some substance if Bulwant Singh was prepared to comment on them. Perhaps I was clutching at straws but, if it were so, we *could* be moving . . . after a long night it was a stimulating thought.

One thing Benjy had said was absolutely right. Most of the vegetation had ceased to steam, and by early afternoon the surface of the airstrip, dazzlingly white under the hot sun, was dry and the wheelmarks powdery in places.

The porous coral had absorbed a huge volume of seawater, yet it seemed to have had little effect on the quality of the drinking water from the wells. There were salt stains on the walls and more brown scorpions in evidence than usual, but it was extraordinary how soon things got back to normal.

Gilbert's liberated fowl had come down from the high branches to peck away between the shrubs. They still had their jaunty attitude, but were now noticeably scrawnier than the survivors of Daya Singh's flock.

The weather was still disturbed and sultry, and during the following week we suffered a more local onslaught by wind and waves. In mid-afternoon a violent storm-cum-waterspout hit the lagoon, drawing up the water and banking it into ridges about the centre of the disturbance.

John Gossard was on Maladu looking at an old well near the beach when, without warning, the storm whipped in with a swirl of heavy greenish cloud and overturned a Maldivian outrigger, just offshore. In it he'd seen two men and a young lad. One clung to the craft while the other was trying to reach the boy, who'd been flung clear. John plunged into the ferocious sea and with his considerable strength managed to bring the boy to the beach. In a matter of minutes the storm centre passed and the others struggled ashore.

John then found himself faced with a rather different ordeal. The Maldivians who regularly visited Maladu insisted, through Martin Welland whom they knew well, on a formal thanksgiving ceremony. The NOIC informed an official Maldivian delegation that he'd host celebrations on Maladu itself at the weekend.

Uncomfortably garlanded, John sat in state under a mango tree outside the old village, a fixed smile on his battered features, as conch shells trumpeted the arrival of each new boatload from Makofulu, fresh faces to be presented to him by the boy he'd rescued. He carried it off well, responding as best he could to the effusive greetings and numerous offerings from the trestle tables laden with rice and fish and sugary sweets, to which, once they'd greeted him, the men in neat white shirts and *longis*, and the women in their best *saris* had made their way.

Captain Turner's elderly seniority induced sufficient respect for him to make a concluding speech as soon as decently possible and extricate Gossard, ostensibly for another formal ceremony in the Wardroom.

As we bumped gently over the long bridge between the islands, watching the bright family groups leaving the beaches, their billowing sails bobbing on the edge of the tidal race, I felt that our time on the atoll was running out, and that shortly this curious, isolated existence would seem as ephemeral as indeed it was.

CHAPTER FIFTEEN

The Vocation of Bachan Singh

Let every man practise the art he knows best.
Cicero: *Tusculanae disputationes I* (45 BC)

Suddenly on August the Sixth, and then again on the Ninth, the unexpected happened; and, of course, our small world, as well as the wider world, would never be the same again. By the Fourteenth the Japanese had capitulated, and on September the Second they signed the formal instrument of surrender.

But somehow, for us, VJ Day was an anticlimax, compared with VE Day. The party was over, and a new set of circumstances faced us all individually. Someone had pulled the plug, and on the Equator the flow is straight down. We were about to be sucked in and most of us had no idea where we'd be ejected.

The Subedar certainly knew what was facing his own people, now that the days of the Raj were coming to an end and the British about to leave India. He knew that the relationships between himself and his old companion the Subedar Major, Honorary Lieutenant Mohammed Khan, and with so many of the Punjabi Mussalmans he had served with throughout his long career, could never be the same again.

Most of us kept such thoughts well below the surface, so that outwardly there was an end-of-term atmosphere about it all. No one had been posted back yet, though Bill Forrest-Hill was already handing out his cards, with a West End Theatrical Club address on one side and a Richmond address scored through and defaced dramatically by the word "flattened" on the other. Smivvy, too, was full of ideas about the future, mostly aimed at exploiting the possibilities of central London.

The rest of us, even established family men like John Gossard and Philip Shuttleworth, were less certain. Gilbert and Box were making tentative plans to resume University life, of one sort or another, though as it turned out the three of us would have many months of soldiering still ahead of us.

The Order to return to India came a few weeks later; but by that time I knew that I'd be leaving the Company as soon as we were back at Depot and would part from Box and the rest of them, and return to England after all the years of separation from home and family.

It was an odd feeling, for almost every contact within the Company became a poignant one. When Prem Singh, that efficient self-effacing Company Clerk brought in the mail from the Catalina, I knew I would miss him a great deal. Signing the book after the last of the *arzi* parades, which had given one such an insight into the hopes and fears of the people we would soon be leaving behind, was like closing the door of a Club to which there would be no further admission.

The VCOs, of course, would go their own ways, as would such characters as Hen Keeper Daya Singh and the ever-optimistic gardener Kirpal Singh, who'd played lesser parts but had fitted so well into Company life. There'd be sad partings from the orderlies, from Karam Singh, who'd never put a foot wrong, and from gangling Ajit Singh. I shall always picture Ajit Singh as he sat in the MLC as we left the shore, one hand on his kit and the other on Furry, who was sitting on the Company clock, as he'd done when we'd arrived.

The greatest sense of loss was to come, of course, with my farewell to the Subedar. The final parting from Bulwant Singh took place nearly a month after we'd left the atoll, when late one evening we walked together by the Mula river . . . and exchanged our gifts.

There was, however, one splendid moment, a day or two before we left the atoll. An incident which was the perfect way to bring down the curtain on this strangely unreal period at the tail-end of it all. Which is why it's as well to take leave of 725 Independent Engineer Company, not as the men dispersed back in the old Training Battalion, but while it was still on Manu, with a day or so of its island life still to run.

Once again it was packing time and carting time. Box had just left Pritap Singh by the Stores and was waving in my direction. It seemed urgent, so I hurried towards him; but he put his fingers to his lips and

I slowed down. He was pointing to something beyond the huts, towards the airstrip.

There on the edge of the clearing was a line of goats, eight of them, all that remained of Bachan Singh's charges. They walked in bright sunshine, nose to tail, slowly ambling towards the shady path which curves away through the bushes. As we watched, the stocky, bandy-legged, would-be soldier drew himself up and barked his words of command . . . 'Halt!' and all the goats stopped . . . 'Queek March!' and with military precision they moved off, not in step, though in line, and on up the path . . . followed by Bachan Singh.